"You made all t[...]

Kathryn ducked her head shyly. "I even hooked the rug."

Impressed, Jake lifted his eyebrows. This was a woman of immense talent. "I suppose you painted the cabinets in the kitchen, too."

"Who else? There's no one here but me."

"I thought you lived with your mom."

Kathryn dipped her chin, dropping her gaze. "I—I did. She passed ten months ago, and before that she was far too immobile to stencil cabinets."

Jake let that sink in. After a moment, he muttered, "We ought to get on our way."

He mused that, if things went well with the shop, maybe he and Frankie could find their own place and hire Kathryn Stepp to decorate it.

Suddenly an idea sprang into his mind. What if he could convince his brother to hire Kathryn? Jake would benefit from this, too.

At least that was what he told himself.

It was a far more comfortable thought than the idea that he might like having Kathryn Stepp around the ranch.

Arlene James has been publishing steadily for nearly four decades and is a charter member of RWA. She is married to an acclaimed artist, and together they have traveled extensively. After growing up in Oklahoma, Arlene lived thirty-four years in Texas and now abides in beautiful northwest Arkansas, near two of the world's three loveliest, smartest, most talented granddaughters. She is heavily involved in her family, church and community.

Books by Arlene James

Love Inspired

Three Brothers Ranch

The Rancher's Answered Prayer
Rancher to the Rescue

The Prodigal Ranch

The Rancher's Homecoming
Her Single Dad Hero
Her Cowboy Boss

Chatam House

Anna Meets Her Match
A Match Made in Texas
Baby Makes a Match
An Unlikely Match
Second Chance Match
Building a Perfect Match

Visit the Author Profile page at Harlequin.com for more titles.

Rancher
to the Rescue

Arlene James

HARLEQUIN® LOVE INSPIRED®

Recycling programs
for this product may
not exist in your area.

LOVE INSPIRED BOOKS

ISBN-13: 978-1-335-47903-7

Rancher to the Rescue

www.Harlequin.com

Printed in U.S.A.

As for God, his way is perfect;
the word of the Lord is tried: he is a buckler
to all them that trust in him.
—*2 Samuel* 22:31

For Pattie Steele-Perkins.
You've always had my back,
and I can't thank you enough.
God bless you, my friend.

Chapter One

Glancing at his three-year-old in the rearview mirror of the double cab pickup truck, Jake cranked up the air-conditioning.

"Sorry, son. It's just too hot to ride with the windows down."

Frankie made a face, but said nothing as Jake hit the buttons that rolled up the windows. The boy loved the wind in his face, even the scorching wind of an August morning, which was one reason he'd taken off at a heady gallop on his pony across the field after his six-year-old cousin yesterday. Tyler was a more experienced rider than Frankie, and Jake's heart had leaped into his throat as he'd watched his son's dark head bouncing along behind his nephew's horse. Thankfully, Jake had caught up to him before the boy had lost his seat.

Determined that both the boy and the pony would receive further instruction before being allowed out of the corral again, Jake had brought Frankie along with him while he ran errands. He didn't have any other option. His brothers, Wyatt and Ryder, and Wyatt's son, Tyler, were out on horseback checking the least-accessible water holes on the ranch, and Wyatt's wife, Tina, had a doctor's appointment.

Given the size and population of his native Houston, Jake had always thought that in Texas, it was a long drive to get anywhere, but Oklahoma was proving its equal. Its many small towns and few big cities were separated by long stretches of empty road. Consequently, Oklahoma felt rather lonely to Jake, even more so since Wyatt had married Tyler's mother in June.

Tina and Tyler were good for his brother, and Jake wished them only happiness, but now that Wyatt had his own family, Jake had started to feel out of place at Loco Man Ranch. He and his two brothers had spent many joyous summers running wild over the two thousand acres of the ranch on the outskirts of tiny War Bonnet before inheriting the place from their uncle Dodd a few months ago. More and more, though, Jake felt like an interloper in his sister-in-law's house and an unnecessary dependent on the ranching enterprise. As a mechanic, trained by the army, Jake felt the ranch simply did not need or maintain enough vehicles to keep him busy or justify his take of the profits, which were irregular.

On the other hand, the nearest mechanic to War Bonnet was at least thirty miles away. Jake figured he could pull in enough business from the surrounding countryside to turn a profit. So, right after the wedding, with the blessings of his brothers and sister-in-law, Jake had the foundation poured for a shop that he was building at the very edge of the road fronting the ranch property, only a few hundred yards from the house. While doing much of the building himself and keeping a close eye on his budget, he was quickly acquiring building materials and inventory. If the shop was up and running within the next month or so, he should have enough of his dwindling savings left to see him through until the business fulfilled expectations.

With his mind full of lists and plans, he didn't notice the old car beside the road until he was right on it. A woman was bent over the front fender of the little coupe, her head hidden by the raised hood, one tennis shoe kicked up into the air and her long full skirt rising to the backs of her knees. Jake knew instantly that he had to stop. Already hotter than ninety degrees with a high in triple digits predicted, it was too hot to be stranded on the side of the road, and out here the next vehicle might be long in coming.

He brought the big pickup truck to a grinding halt beside the two-lane pavement, well ahead of the stranded car. Shifting the transmission into Park with one hand, he rolled down all the windows with the other before killing the engine. "Don't you get out of your seat," he instructed Frankie. "I'll be right back. I'm just going to help this lady."

Frankie leaned forward and craned his neck, looking behind them. "What lady?"

"Don't know," Jake replied, reaching for the pale straw cowboy hat on the passenger seat. "Looks like her car broke down."

He got out, settled his hat on his head and pushed his sunshades farther up on his nose, wishing he'd taken the time to shave that morning. The coal-dark dusting of beard on his cheeks, jaws and upper lip always made him look rough and undisciplined, or so his late wife, Jolene, had said. He didn't want to scare this poor woman any more than she likely already was.

Jolene, like him, had been military. If she hadn't died in a training accident, they'd still be soldiers together, army from the tops of their heads to the soles of their feet. That was a tough life for a single father, however.

He approached the hissing car with a smile for a greeting, only to find that his damsel in distress had retreated into her vehicle. Lifting his eyebrows, he casually strolled up to the driver's window and tapped on the glass.

"Howdy." He gestured to the raised hood of her car. "Got a little trouble, I see. How about I take a look?"

For a long moment, she just stared at him with wide, forest green eyes. Then she folded in her lips and bit them. Finally, she rolled down the window a half inch or so.

"I don't know you."

He put out his hand. "Jacoby Smith, from Loco Man Ranch. Most folks call me Jake."

She didn't lower the window. Instead, she stared at him, biting her lips in what was obviously a nervous habit. He gestured toward the hood of her car again.

"I'm going to take a look." Without giving her a chance to object, he stepped to the front of the car and began to take stock. "Can you start it?"

After a moment, she turned the key. It didn't take long for him to diagnose the problem. He went to the window again, finding that she'd lowered it all the way, finally.

Fanning herself with her hand, she spoke before he had a chance to do so. "I suppose you're Dodd's kin."

"That's right. He was our uncle."

She stopped fanning and squinted up at him. "I was sorry to hear he'd passed."

"Thanks. My brothers and I were fond of the old boy."

"You'd be one of those three nephews who used to spend summers with him, then."

"Right again. And you are?"

"Fine," she said quickly. "I'm fine." Her dusky pink lips formed the words even as her gaze cut to the hood of her car. "Just need some water for the radiator, I think."

Jake shook his head, irritated that she wouldn't give him her name. Unlike so many others he'd met in the area, she wasn't exactly a friendly sort, but she needed help. More than she knew.

"I think you've blown a head gasket. At least."

"You can't possibly know that for sure," she scoffed, a hint of desperation in her voice.

"I've seen it many times. I happen to be a mechanic."

She made a face, as if to say that only made his opinion more suspect.

"Look," he snapped, "I'm not out here trying to drum up business."

"Then why'd you stop?" she shot back, turning her head away. "You don't know me."

Recognizing the sound of impending tears, Jake pulled in a slow, calming breath. "I stopped," he said evenly, "because no one should be left stranded beside the road in this heat. Is there anyone you can call for a lift?"

She thought for a minute, biting her lips, and shook her head.

He raised his hands, palms up, in a gesture meant to convey that they were out of options. "My son and I will be glad to give you a ride."

Sniffing, she eyed him suspiciously. "I didn't see anyone else in the truck."

"He's three," Jake gritted out, reaching deep for patience. "You ought to be able to see the top of his car seat at least."

She stuck her head out the window and studied the truck. Her thick, dark gold hair parted in the middle of her head and swung in a jaunty, ragged flip two or three inches above her shoulders. Sinking into the car again, she tucked the sun-kissed strands behind a dainty ear and muttered, "Oh, yes. I see that now."

Heat radiated up off the pavement in blistering waves. Jake pushed back the brim of his hat. "We can take you wherever you need to go."

She lifted her chin, swallowing hard and exposing her long, sleek neck and the delicate skin of her throat in the process. Jake's chest tightened. He told himself it was concern, the fear that she was going to send him away, though he was her only immediate source of help. During his first deployment, he'd developed the habit of speaking silently to the Lord in moments of need, and this was one of those moments.

Lord, You'd better zap some sense into her. It's not safe for her to sit out here in this heat. Even worse if she tries to walk wherever she's headed.

To his relief, she slowly opened the car door and got out, slinging a large fabric bag over one shoulder. She was taller than he'd expected, and her blouse, worn over a full gray skirt, was of the medical variety, like the top half of a scrub suit. A muted green, it crisscrossed in front and tied at the side, creating a V neckline that exposed a dainty but prominent collarbone.

"In case you forgot, my name's Jacoby Smith. Jake."

"Jake," she whispered in acknowledgment. "Kathryn Stepp."

"Nice to meet you, Kathryn, despite the circumstances. Now, shall we?" He nodded at the truck. Reluctantly, her arms folded across her middle, she began to walk in that direction. Shortening his steps to keep pace with her, he asked, "Where can I take you?"

She bit her lips before saying, "I—I need to get to a client's house. Sandy Cabbot. He'll be wanting his lunch soon."

"Don't know him. How do I get there?"

"Just head on east to the county line, then go left. It's only a few miles."

"No problem. You'll have to point out this county line to me, though."

She seemed surprised by that. "Oh. All right."

They drew alongside the truck. Jake opened the front passenger door for her and jerked his thumb toward the back seat. "That's my boy, Frankie."

Frankie waved at her. She waved back, smiling timidly, before climbing into the truck. Jake walked around, tossed his hat onto the back seat next to Frankie and slid behind the steering wheel in time to see her pass a trembling hand over her forehead.

He started the engine and rolled up the windows, sitting for a moment to let the cool air from the vents flow over them. "Tough morning, I take it."

She nodded. He waited. After a long moment, she softly said, "Without that car, I can't work, and if I can't work, I can't fix the car or…" She shrugged morosely.

"I find things usually look better if we give them some time," Jake told her, getting the truck underway.

Muttering something about time running out, she pulled a cell phone from the pocket of her voluminous skirt. "I have to make a phone call." He listened unapologetically as she placed the call and spoke into the phone. "Sandy, this is Kathryn again. I've got a ride. See you in a few minutes."

She replaced the phone in her pocket then jerked when Frankie yelled, "Hey, lady!"

Jake briefly closed his eyes. His outgoing, energetic three-year-old didn't take well to being ignored, and he habitually spoke at the top of his lungs. Tina claimed that was perfectly normal. Applying patience, Jake prepared to remind Frankie to use his "inside voice." Before he had the chance, Kathryn Stepp twisted and gazed into the back seat.

"Hello."

"Hay-ell-o!" Frankie repeated happily, mimicking her Oklahoma drawl.

Jake winced, but she laughed. "You're a cutie."

"You a cutie!" Frankie bellowed back at her.

"Take it down a notch, please," Jake instructed.

She glanced at Jake but went on speaking to Frankie. "Are you having fun, riding around with Daddy today?"

"No," Frankie said bluntly, moderating his volume a bit. "I wanna ride my pony."

She frowned. "That sounds dangerous. Doesn't your mama worry you'll get hurt when you ride your pony?"

Jake leaned forward slightly, watching his son's face in the rearview mirror.

Frankie replied matter-of-factly. "No. She in heben."

"Heaven," Jake corrected gently, relaxing into his seat again.

"Oh," Kathryn said, sobering. "I'm sorry."

"She like it," Frankie said, sounding unconcerned.

"That's nice." Turning to Jake, she asked, "He's only three?"

"About three and a half."

"He seems big for his age," she commented, as if that were a worrisome thing.

"Smiths are big men," Jake muttered defensively.

At the same time, Frankie asked, "S'wat her name?" He often got his contractions backward, substituting *s'wat* for *what's* and *s'that* for *that's*.

"It's Miss Stepp." Or so Jake assumed. Surely if she had a husband, she'd have called him for help. On the other hand, maybe the man was out of town. Glancing at her, he asked, "Or is it missus?"

She bit her lips before answering coolly, "Miss."

Couldn't say he was surprised. She didn't seem to trust men. Or was it that she just didn't like or trust him?

She was a pretty woman, though, with that long, long neck and those intense green eyes and rosy lips. Obviously, she didn't take much stock in her appearance, given her mismatched garb, straggly hair and utter lack of cosmetics. Even Jolene had known how to get dressed up.

His late wife had been the perfect soldier, but once the uniform had come off, she'd tended toward sparkles and slinky fabrics. He'd often wondered if that had been her way of making up for her dedication to all things military. This quiet, nervous female hardly seemed of the same species. If Jolene's transportation

had broken down beside the road, she'd have comman-
deered the first vehicle to cross her path.

He supposed that most women would be more cautious. Few had Jolene's training and confidence, and
too many men were willing to take advantage of a
woman alone, especially a timid one. Glad that he'd
stopped, even if this unexpected passenger was prickly,
Jake smiled at her. Instantly, she leaned away from him,
her eyes going wide.

So much for chivalry.

Kathryn had never known how to behave around
men, especially the good-looking ones, and Jake
Smith definitely fit into that category. With his rumpled black-coffee-colored hair, chiseled features and
straight white teeth, he was movie-star handsome, and
that dark, prickly shadow practically shouted masculin-
ity. It was the way he moved that made her so nervous,
however. Every motion proclaimed him a confident,
capable man who had never met an obstacle he couldn't
overcome.

Before getting into the vehicle with him, she'd rea-
soned that no man with a three-year-old in tow would
truly present a threat, but old habits died hard. Since
the age of seventeen, Kathryn had been virtually on
her own, apart from the wider world, tied to her mom's
bedside by that woman's debilitating physical condi-
tion. Always shy, Kathryn had never been very brave
or confident, and from the time of her mother's accident, she had diligently taken every precaution, especially after her father had abandoned them.

As usual, thoughts of Mitchel Stepp brought a world
of worry down on Kathryn. How was she to keep him

from forcing the sale of her home when she couldn't come up with the money to buy him out? And now her car was broken down. If only she could find her mother's insurance policy. It wouldn't pay much, but it might be enough to satisfy her father for at least a while. Her salary as a home care provider covered her bills and allowed her to put aside a bit every month to cover the property taxes that would come due at the end of the year, but Mitchel expected thousands, half the value of her house.

As Jake pulled the metallic olive-green truck to a stop in front of Sandy Cabbot's lonely little farmhouse, he glanced around. "Can someone here give you a ride back to town when you're finished? I don't see a car anywhere."

Shaking her head, she opened the door. "I'll manage. Thanks for your help."

"It's no problem," he said. "If you want me to look at your car—"

She cut that off right away. "I can't afford to pay you, Mr. Smith."

He balanced a forearm against the top of the steering wheel. "Jake. I didn't ask for payment. And the fact is you can't go walking far in this heat."

Stepping out onto the running board, she replied, "We do what we must." That was one lesson she'd learned early and well.

"What time are you through here?" he asked.

She reached the ground and turned to face him. "Why?"

He pulled off his mirrored shades and tossed them onto the dash, fixing her with a hard stare. His eyes were such a dark brown they were almost black. "What time?"

"Six." The reply was out before she could stop it.

"Then I'll be back at six."

Kathryn bit her lips. She knew she shouldn't get in that truck with him again. He made her feel…well, not frightened really, but completely inadequate, and she did not need help with that. She cleared her throat anxiously. "That's not—"

He reached across and pulled the cab door shut.

"—necessary," she muttered, watching as he backed the truck around and drove away in a cloud of red dust.

Confident, capable, commanding—and apparently not used to taking no for an answer—he was exactly the last sort of man she should find attractive, and that she did find him attractive, wildly so, was reason enough to avoid him. She didn't know how to deal with a man like him, but then he wouldn't be interested in a plain, shy, unsophisticated woman like her, anyway. At least she wouldn't have to walk back to town tonight. How she'd manage tomorrow, she couldn't imagine, but she'd worry about that, and everything else, later. Moving toward the house, she thought of the boy and smiled.

Hey, lady.

Frankie certainly wasn't shy. She didn't know anything about children, but despite losing his mother at such a tender age, he seemed to be happy and well-adjusted, if a bit loud. Nevertheless, with her own mother's death still fresh in her memory, her heart went out to him.

She wondered what had happened to the late Mrs. Smith. Illness or accident? Mia Stepp's death had been a combination of the two, her illness a direct result of the automobile accident that had battered her body and left her paralyzed and brain damaged. Kathryn missed her dreadfully, but Frankie's confident, carefree words concerning his own mother came back to her.

She in heben. She like it.

Kathryn prayed that was so. For both his mother and hers.

As she greeted Sandy, her elderly client, and began checking his vital signs before starting his lunch, she couldn't help wondering how long ago Mrs. Jake Smith had passed on. And how many women were already lined up to take her place.

It made no difference. She would never see Jake Smith again after this evening.

She certainly would not think of him as her rescuer.

Even if he was.

Chapter Two

Despite Frankie's many questions, Jake couldn't get Kathryn Stepp off his mind. *You'd think no one had ever done that woman a favor before*, Jake mused as he wandered around the auto parts store, waiting for the clerk to bring up his supplies from the warehouse. It cost less for the supplier to ship his goods to the auto parts store in Ardmore than to the ranch.

"S'wat that?" Frankie pointed at a rotating display rack.

"Air freshener. It makes the car smell good."

"I wan' it." Frankie reached out his hand.

Jake took the inexpensive air freshener from the display. In the shape of a fir tree, it smelled of evergreen. He scratched the odor patch on the back of the package and held it to Frankie's nose. The boy inhaled deeply, smiled and nodded.

"Okay, but after it's opened it stays in the truck. It's not a toy."

Nodding, Frankie reached for the package. Jake handed it over. Frankie immediately reached for another. "Ty'er want one," he said.

Jake picked up another air freshener for Tyler. They continued wandering the store until the clerk signaled them a few moments later.

After loading boxes into the bed of the truck, they stopped for lunch then ran two more errands before heading home. As Jake turned toward the ranch, he thought of Kathryn Stepp again, of the tears she'd tried to hide from him and the worry in her voice.

Without that car, I can't work, and if I can't work, I can't fix the car. I can't afford to pay you, Mr. Smith.

Mr. Smith.

The contrary woman didn't like him much, though he was just trying to help her. She did like Frankie, though, and vice versa. That counted with Jake. Besides, how could he not help when he had the skills to do so?

For most of the drive, he mulled over how to convince her to accept his assistance. Maybe Tina could talk Kathryn into letting him work on her car. Or the Billings sisters. The Billingses were a prominent ranching family around War Bonnet, greatly respected for their honesty and generosity. He wondered if he could get Tina to ride with him when he went to pick up Kathryn that evening. It would be an inconvenience. Six was the dinner hour in the Smith household. Why couldn't Kathryn Stepp just accept his help and let that be that?

Before he could decide how to handle the problem, he came upon her old car. Instinctively, he whipped over to the shoulder of the road and got out. A quick look told him that the little coupe had a standard transmission and the door was unlocked. Jake kept a sturdy chain handy for emergencies such as this. It was the work of minutes to hook up the chain, flick on the flashers and move the car's transmission out of gear so he could tow it.

"The lady's car!" Frankie exclaimed gleefully as Jake slowly tugged the little old coupe into motion.

"Yep. The lady's car," Jake confirmed, feeling the snap and tug of the chain.

Towing a car like this was risky business, but if he slowed properly he could bring both vehicles to a halt without causing damage to either. He guided the truck and coupe into a slow, arcing turn and made his way to Loco Man Ranch on the outskirts of War Bonnet, where he coasted to a stop in the middle of the compound yard. The coupe came to a rest right behind Tina's old car.

Tina was driving a brand-spanking-new SUV now, and Ryder was supposed to be driving Tina's car, but Jake had noticed that his little brother found lots of excuses for driving his brothers' trucks instead. He couldn't blame Ryder. All the Smith brothers stood three inches over six feet, and Ryder was by far the biggest, most muscular of the trio. A small car wasn't a good fit.

Jake took Frankie and their purchases into the house, where Frankie instantly announced, "We got a lady an'er car!"

Tina, who was removing the lunch dishes from the newly installed dishwasher, straightened in surprise. "I need to go shopping more often. What size lady did you get?"

Jake chuckled. "We stopped to help a lady whose car broke down beside the road. I towed it into the yard so I can take a look at it."

"Oh. Good thing you happened along. Where's the lady?"

"I took her to work. Gotta go back and get her at six."

"Ah. I can go get her if you want," Tina offered lightly. "If you don't mind eating early."

He shrugged as if it didn't matter. But somehow, it did. "I'll take care of it. Besides, I need to talk to her about her car." Tina nodded, but for some reason, Jake felt as if he needed to defend himself. "She doesn't seem to have much money."

Tina smiled. "Naturally you'll help her."

He didn't know what to say to that, so he changed the subject. "Frankie's got something for Tyler. To go in the new SUV."

"Christmas tree!" Frankie declared, holding the two small packages aloft.

"So that's why you had to have it." Jake chuckled. "You're four months too early, pal."

Smiling, Tina went to take Frankie's arm. "Tyler's in his room. Let's carry it up to him. Okay?"

Frankie nodded happily, and they moved toward the hallway.

"If you don't mind keeping an eye on him for a little while," Jake said quickly, "I'd like to get Kathryn's car into the barn and go over it."

Tina shot him a smile over one shoulder. "Sure. And thanks for picking up those things for me."

"No problem."

As he headed to the door, Jake heard her say to Frankie, "Kathryn, hmm?"

"*Miss* Kat'ryn," Frankie corrected.

Tina's soft *hmm* made Jake wince.

Newlyweds always thought everyone around them was trying to couple up. Well, he'd been there and done that already. Besides, even if he dared reach for such happiness again, he suspected that once in a life-time was all anyone could expect. Maybe it was all he could endure.

"Where's Frankie?" Kathryn asked, trying not to sound as nervous as she felt.

"Playing with his cousin."

The truck engine idling, Jake waited patiently until she buckled her seat belt before backing the truck around and heading it down the dirt road.

Kathryn watched Sandy's little house recede in the side-view mirror of the truck and wondered if she'd ever be back, and if not, what would become of the gaunt, pleasant old man. Nearly ninety, he got around with the help of a walker and in the average week saw just Kathryn and a rural nurse. With his family far away, he depended on professional caregivers.

Out of the blue, Jake Smith said, "I towed your car to Loco Man."

She gasped. "You did *what*? I told you, I can't af-ford—"

"Yeah, yeah, I get it," he interrupted, shaking a hand at her. "But I couldn't leave it sitting on the side of the road. It could've been hit. And I don't know where you live, so I couldn't tow it there. Besides, I can fix it for the cost of the parts. My shop's not operational yet, but I've got everything I need to work on it in the barn."

Hope welled up inside her. "You'd do that?"

"Sure. I can give you wholesale prices on the

parts, too, but it's still gonna cost in the hundreds," he warned. "The engine has to be completely rebuilt."

Her hope of a moment before waned. If only she could find that insurance policy, but she'd looked everywhere she could think to look. The company insisted that they had no record of the changes they'd agreed upon more than a decade ago. Kathryn bit her lips, noticed him watching and stopped. A moment's thought told her she really had no other choice.

"Put together an estimate then," she told him uncertainly. "I'll try to figure out something." Hopefully, her tax savings would cover it. If not…she didn't want to go there.

"I'll calculate the estimate tonight," he promised. "Now, where am I taking you?"

"Oh. It's Sixth Street. Number eleven. In War Bonnet, of course."

They drove along in silence for some time before he abruptly announced that Frankie had begged for air fresheners for himself and his cousin because they came in the shape of Christmas trees. Kathryn had to digest that.

"You mean those evergreen car fresheners?"

"Yep."

"You know those could be dangerous, don't you? He shouldn't put it in his mouth."

"Relax, worrywart," Jake said, grinning. "The air fresheners are still in their packages, and once they come out, they'll be used for their intended purpose."

"Oh. Well, you can't be too careful."

"Really? You mean like accepting rides from strangers on isolated Oklahoma roads?"

She started to say that she hadn't had any other

choice, but suddenly every murder mystery she'd ever read, every cop show she'd ever watched, flitted through her mind.

"Oh, come on," Jake said. "You're perfectly safe with me. It was a joke."

Kathryn caught a swift breath and provided him with a weak smile. "I'm sure I am. It's just that this has never happened before, and I can't help worrying. A-about the car."

"Want me to stop off at the ranch and ask my sister-in-law to ride the rest of the way with us?" he asked, clearly not fooled.

She considered it, but Sandy knew where she was and who she was with. He spent a great deal of time on the phone with his few remaining friends, and word had filtered through the grapevine that the Smith brothers were regular attenders at Countryside Church and friends of the Billings family. Besides, Jake had been very generous with his time and concern thus far. She shook her head, feeling a little foolish.

"No. Thanks for offering, though."

He smiled, nodded and fell silent again.

It's just that he's so handsome, she told herself, *and so big*.

She was used to standing as tall as most men, or nearly so. Those she met in the grocery store and at the gas station weren't usually as tall as him. Plus, she knew them, at least by sight or name, and if they spoke to her, she just nodded and moved on. Glancing at Jake's broad, long-fingered hands, she wondered why none of those other men seemed as strong, capable or dangerous as him. She felt a keen sense of relief—and a puzzling disappointment—when they turned onto Sixth Street.

"This is a lovely part of town," he remarked, slowly navigating the tree-shaded lane.

"Yes. Our house is the smallest on the street, but it's so pretty here."

"Our?" he queried. The word came out sharply.

"It's my mother's house," she murmured, deciding not to mention her mother's recent death. Of course, he could find out from anybody in town, but why would he? Whether he was a Good Samaritan or merely drumming up business, his only interest would be in her car. He was no threat and couldn't have any interest in her personally. Still, she owed him no explanations.

He brought the big truck to a halt in the narrow drive, glancing around. "This is really nice."

Kathryn couldn't help smiling. She was proud of her flower beds, and she thought the green trim, which matched the shingles on the roof, made a pretty contrast to the white siding.

"About the car," he said, abruptly switching subjects. "When should I drop off the estimate?"

She didn't stop to wonder why he didn't offer to call with the estimate. "I have to be at a client's house every morning by ten and don't get off until six."

How she was going to get to her clients, she had no idea. Sandy had suggested she rent a car from a facility in Ardmore, but a quick telephone call had revealed that even a few days' rental fee would consume more of her income than she could afford, and it wouldn't fix her car. Maybe the agency for which she worked could offer a solution. Hopefully, one other than firing her.

Jake nodded. "I see. Okay, then."

She grappled for the door handle, found it and let herself out of the idling truck. "Thank you so much for your help."

Smiling in acknowledgment, he nodded again. She shut the door and stepped back. Within moments, he and his truck had disappeared the way they'd come. As Kathryn turned toward the house, she spied old Mrs. Trident glaring at her from the front steps of the house next door. Kathryn waved, but Mrs. Trident simply turned and went back inside.

She'd avoided the Stepp household since Kathryn's father had stumbled up the wrong steps, drunk and belligerent, one night more than a decade ago. Soon after, realizing that Mia Stepp was never going to recover from her accident, he'd abandoned his handicapped wife and seventeen-year-old daughter, but that didn't seem to matter to Mrs. Trident. In all those years, Kathryn hadn't heard from her father until about six months after her mother's death, when he'd sent a letter demanding that Kathryn sell the house and split the profit with him.

Kathryn started toward her own front door, sighing heavily, but as she traveled along the walkway flanked by daylilies and Shasta daisies, she felt a familiar sense of peace and belonging settle over her. This place had always been her sanctuary, the one safe spot in the whole world. She loved this old house. Living anywhere else seemed unimaginable. Somehow, she had to keep her father from forcing her to sell it. If only she could find that missing insurance policy.

Shaking her head, she pushed aside such thoughts and went indoors to telephone her employer and inform them of her changed circumstances. It wasn't as if that insurance money could save her house, after all. She simply would not think of everything else it could do.

"Pretty!" Frankie declared the next morning, pointing to the wreath hanging on the front door of the Stepp house.

Frankie had said the word half a dozen times since they'd pulled into the driveway. While they waited for someone to answer Jake's knock, Frankie gestured toward the prim white wicker rocking chair on the porch. The ruffles on its flowered cushions fluttered in the breeze.

"I know," Jake said wryly, smiling down at his son, "pretty."

The door opened, and Kathryn Stepp gaped at him with obvious alarm. "What are you doing here?"

Wearing a loose, flowered dress that hung almost to her ankles over slender bare feet, she folded her arms, trying—and failing—to fix a stern expression on her face. She looked like a girl playing dress up, a very pretty if somewhat bedraggled girl.

Jake removed his shades, tucked them into his shirt pocket and doffed his pale straw cowboy hat. "Morning."

Frankie, who knew nothing but exuberance, lurched forward and threw his arms around her, bellowing, "Mording!"

After shooting a shocked, puzzled glance at Jake, Kathryn softened. She leaned forward slightly and returned Frankie's hug as best she could, shuffling her feet to keep her toes from being squashed by his athletic shoes.

"Good morning. What brings you and your daddy here today?"

"We're here to give you a ride to work," Jake answered. Wasn't it obvious? He removed a folded sheet of paper from his hip pocket. "The ride will give you a chance to look over this estimate."

Her rosy lips turned down in a frown. "I'm not sure I have a job to go to. It depends on if they've found someone to replace me already."

"Shouldn't you find out?" Jake asked.

She turned her head, glancing into the room. For the first time, Jake looked past her. The living area was larger than he'd expected, with gleaming wood floors and a painted brick fireplace set against a sage-green interior wall. Colorful throw pillows and a basket of flowers in the center of the coffee table gave the room a cheery note. Clean and bright, the room felt peaceful and welcoming.

Frankie broke free of Kathryn and ran to climb up onto the sofa. "Look, Daddy! Pretty." He patted a throw pillow.

"Very pretty," Jake agreed, chuckling.

Kathryn waved a hand absently. "Uh, come in while I... Come in."

She waited until he stepped inside. Then she closed the door and rushed off down a hallway on the right, calling, "Have a seat! Won't be long!"

Jake removed his hat, but instead of sitting he waited until he heard a door close, then he glanced into the open doorway of what might have been a den but was now a bedroom. Curious, he walked past the hallway and through a dining area filled with dark, ornate furniture. Peeking into the kitchen, he saw Formica countertops, worn white in places, and rusty chips in the enamel on the sink. The appliances had certainly seen better days, and a few of the stenciled doors on the cabinet hung at a tilt that made him want to reach for a screwdriver and hammer. A vase of daisies stood on the windowsill above the sink.

Jake suddenly thought of his mom, how she had placed feminine little touches all around their Houston home. Those delicate, homey traces had gradually disappeared over the years after her death. Jake walked back into the living room and sank down in the easy chair, his hat in his lap.

"Mizz Kat'ryn gots lotta flowers." Frankie pronounced *flowers* as flou-hers.

"Yes, she does."

"I like flowers."

"Me, too."

"Mizz Kat'ryn gotta dog?"

"I don't know."

Frankie had been lobbying for a dog of his own ever since Tyler had gotten his pup a couple months earlier. Recently, Stark Burns, the local veterinarian, had shown them a promising litter. Anxious to acquire his own dog, Frankie didn't understand that the puppies still needed weeks before they could be weaned.

A door opened and footsteps sounded, growing louder until Kathryn appeared, dressed in comfortable blue jeans and a filmy, flowered blouse worn beneath the familiar scrub suit top. Frankie flew toward her and threw his arms around her hips, knocking her back a step.

"Whoa." She still looked sad and worried, though she patted his back.

Frankie beamed up at her. "You gotta dog?"

"Uh, no, afraid not." She looked to Jake and changed the subject. "I can work today. They haven't reassigned my clients yet."

Yet.

"Sounds like you could be out of a job."

"I'm afraid so. At least until my car's fixed."

Jake got to his feet. "Ready when you are."

She went to a closet, opened the door and removed the familiar fabric bag.

Meanwhile, Frankie ran and hopped on the couch again, bouncing slightly. "S'let stay here, Daddy."

Jake shook his head. "Can't. We have to take Miss Kathryn to work."

Leaning back against the pillows, Frankie whined, "I wanna stay."

Nodding, Jake glanced around again. "I understand. It's very nice."

Kathryn closed the closet door. "Thank you, but it's just homemade, secondhand stuff."

"Homemade?"

She shrugged. "Doesn't make good sense to throw away things when a little time and effort can turn them into treasures. A torn sheet makes a fine slipcover or set of throw pillows."

"You made all this?" Jake asked, swirling a hand to encompass the room.

She ducked her head shyly. "I even hooked the rug."

Impressed, Jake lifted his eyebrows. This was a woman of immense talent. "I suppose you painted the cabinets in the kitchen, too."

She looked a little taken aback that he'd seen her

kitchen, but after a moment she said, "Who else? There's no one here but me."

Surprised, Jake tilted his head. "I thought you lived with your mom."

Kathryn dipped her chin, dropping her gaze. "I—I did. She passed ten months ago, and before that she was far too handicapped to stencil cabinets. Or do much of anything else."

Jake let that sink in, frowning at the implications. After a moment, he lifted a hand, muttering, "We ought to get on our way."

Nodding, she followed him and a reluctant Frankie from the house. As he got Frankie settled in the truck, Jake mused that if things went well with the shop, maybe he and Frankie could find their own place and hire Kathryn Stepp to decorate it.

Hire Kathryn Stepp.

An idea sprang into his mind. What if he could convince Wyatt and Tina to hire Kathryn? Tina could certainly use the help getting the ranch house ready for guests. She'd intended to open a bed-and-breakfast in the ranch house from the beginning, and they were already turning away those who wanted to visit relatives in the area. Even if they would only agree to take on Kathryn part-time, that would give her some income.

Realizing that he could say nothing to Kathryn until he'd prayed about this and talked to his brother and sister-in-law, Jake began to marshal his thoughts and put together his arguments. Excited to think that he might have found a solution to Kathryn's problems that would also help Tina prepare the ranch house for guests, he bit back a smile.

He would benefit from this, too. One way or another, he had to fix Kathryn's car. Donating his labor was no issue, but paying for the parts himself would take a bite out of his savings, if she would even let him do it. He doubted she would accept that much charity.

At least that's what he told himself.

It was a far more comfortable thought than the idea that he might like having Kathryn Stepp around the ranch.

Chapter Three

Kathryn folded the list of parts needed to repair her car and slipped it into the bag at her knee, biting her lips. Jake drove in silence for several moments, waiting for her to comment.

"I   I can cover some of this," she admitted shakily, "but I'd have to pay out the rest."

"We can arrange that."

"It could take some time."

"We'll figure it out."

"How long do you think the repairs will take?"

"Depends on how much time I have to work on it and how quickly I can find all the parts. Three, four weeks, at least." He'd hoped to be well on his way to opening his shop by then, but now he'd have to divide his time between building the shop and working on her car. Seeing the tears that shimmered in her eyes, he said nothing of his own concerns.

"I asked the agency to hold my job, but I doubt they will. Reliable transportation is part of the employment contract."

"Things will work out. We can arrange rides for a while."

She shifted uncertainly in her seat. "Oh, I couldn't ask—"

"In fact," he went on, as if she hadn't spoken, "I'd be pleased to offer you a ride to prayer meeting tonight."

Eyes wide, mouth ajar, she looked as if he'd reached out and slapped her. "Uh, no thank you. That is…" She turned red in the face. "I d-don't think it's a good idea."

For *him* to take her to prayer meeting, she meant. At least that was his assumption. He couldn't figure out why she disliked him so much. He'd done his best to be gentlemanly and helpful. Well, if she didn't like him, she didn't like him. So be it. Still, she needed help, and Frankie was absolutely taken with her, so Jake would do his best.

This second client lived even farther from town than her first one. After they arrived at the elderly woman's house, Kathryn thanked him, shouldered her bag and got out of the truck. Frankie began slapping his palm against his window and calling to her.

"Mizz Kat'ryn! Mizz Kat'ryn!"

Jake rolled down the window. Kathryn leaned inside, saying, "Bye, Frankie."

To Jake's surprise, Frankie smacked a big kiss on her cheek. "Bye-bye!"

Smiling, Kathryn threaded an arm through the window and hugged him. "Have a great day."

"Hab gread day!" Frankie called as she hurried into the house. He sighed as if quite satisfied with himself.

Shaking his head, Jake rolled up the window and drove back toward the ranch, wondering why Frankie was so fixated on her. His sudden affection seemed out of proportion, especially given how much she disliked Jake. Kathryn had made it very clear that she didn't want anything more to do with him than she must. That being the case, he hoped she wouldn't turn down any job offer that came from the Smiths. Then how would she manage the repair of her car?

Jake decided to ask Tina to pick up Kathryn that evening. Maybe Kathryn would be more comfortable dealing with a woman, and getting to know Tina might make her more amenable to him. That way, even if Wyatt and Tina decided against hiring her, maybe Jake would ask her to watch Frankie for a few days. That would give Kathryn a little income and let Frankie spend some time with her.

If only she would agree.

Kathryn stared at the empty road and bit her lips. She'd assumed Jake would return to pick her up at the end of the day, but now that she thought of it, he hadn't said as much. Instead, he'd offered to give her a ride to prayer meeting. Had her refusal to attend the prayer meeting left him with the impression that she didn't need a ride home from work?

Unfortunately a ride was the least of her needs. The agency had called earlier to inform her that they had re-assigned her clients. She was welcome to reapply once she had secured transportation again, but until then, she would be removed from their roster. The fact that she'd expected to lose her job didn't soften the blow.

Suddenly, she spied a trail of dust being thrown up by a vehicle headed her way. She muttered a quick prayer of thanks and waved. To her surprise, as the vehicle barreled closer she saw that it was a large burgundy-red SUV, not the familiar olive-green pickup.

The SUV came to an abrupt stop near her, and a shapely woman with short, stylish, reddish-brown hair leaped out. Wearing jeans and a simple checked blouse with the tail tucked in and the collar turned up, she plucked off her sunshades and smiled.

"Kathryn?"

"Yes."

"I'm Tina Smith. Sorry I'm late. If Jake had given me a little more lead time, I'd have had dinner on the table early enough to keep you from standing out here in the heat."

"Oh. Uh. So Jake isn't coming?"

"He and the rest of the guys are on their way to prayer meeting. I didn't see any reason for all of us to be late."

"Prayer meeting," Kathryn murmured. "I'm sorry. I didn't realize how much I was imposing."

Tina waved her words away. "No, no. Don't worry about it." With that, she got back into the vehicle.

Kathryn didn't know what to do except slide in on the passenger side. "I hate putting you out like this."

Tina waved a hand dismissively and put the SUV in motion.

"I—I don't suppose Jake told you that I live on Sixth Street in War Bonnet, did he?"

"In War Bonnet?" Tina echoed. "Nope. He left out that little detail." She shrugged. "Well, it won't hurt me to miss one prayer meeting."

Katherine winced. "I hate to be the cause of that."

"Well," Tina said cautiously, "you could always go to prayer meeting with me."

Kathryn immediately shook her head. "I'm still in my work clothes."

"You're dressed as well as I am," Tina pointed out.

Kathryn bit her lips. It was just that she hadn't been to church in years. Her mother had required almost constant care, allowing breaks of only minutes to do the shopping and household chores. Years earlier they'd attended Countryside Church together, but Kathryn doubted she'd know anyone there anymore. Still, keeping Tina Smith away from church seemed selfish and ungrateful. At least, Kathryn mused, she'd surrendered to impulse that morning and worn the flowered blouse.

"I guess I'll go to prayer meeting with you. I can remove the uniform top."

Tina beamed at her. "Great! We just might make it on time then."

Kathryn struggled out of the uniform top and stuffed it in her bag before pulling out a brush and going after her hair, raking it back from her forehead to the ends.

"That's a very pretty blouse," Tina said.

"Thanks. It was my mom's."

"It looks new."

"She never got to wear it. Right after she bought it, she was in a serious car wreck."

"I'm so sorry. That's awful."

Kathryn nodded and softly said, "She was paralyzed from the chest down."

"How sad."

For some reason, Kathryn found herself going on. "She had partial use of her left arm, but there were neurological issues, too. She couldn't speak more than the odd word, and for the rest of her life she suffered terrible seizures that choked her and cut off her air."

"Poor thing. I take it she's passed."

"Ten months ago."

"Was she ill for a long time?"

"Just over eleven years."

Tina shook her head. "I can't imagine how difficult that must have been."

"Very difficult," Kathryn admitted, "especially after my father left, but I learned what to do."

"Your father left, so you cared for her yourself?"

"Every day."

"How old were you?"

"Seventeen when the accident happened. You'd be surprised how much I miss her. But at least caring for her gave me the skills to find work after she was gone. Honestly, I have no regrets."

"You shouldn't," Tina said fervently. "What a wonderful daughter you are. Your mom had to know that."

Blushing, Kathryn dropped her gaze. "That's nice of you to say."

"No wonder Jake is so concerned for you."

Kathryn's gaze zipped right back up to Tina's profile. "Oh, Jake doesn't know. I mean, we haven't discussed it."

"No? Huh. Well, he is concerned, and he'll help if you let him." She glanced at Kathryn. "But that's the Smith brothers for you."

For the rest of the drive, Tina regaled Kathryn with the story of how she'd met the Smith brothers and married the eldest one. Clearly, she was wild about Wyatt Smith. "Jake's the most wonderful father," she enthused as she parked the SUV in the church lot. "We can thank Frankie for that. Isn't he the most adorable kid?"

"He is," Kathryn agreed, getting out of the vehicle when Tina did.

"I think Frankie is why Wyatt so easily accepts my son," Tina went on, coming around to meet Kathryn. "Wyatt took care of Frankie when Jake and Jolene were deployed."

"Deployed?"

Taking her arm, Tina turned Kathryn toward the building. They fell in step as they moved toward the door. "They were both career army. Didn't you know? I don't think Jake would ever have taken discharge if his wife hadn't died."

"I see." The poor man. Kathryn bit her lips, but she couldn't keep herself from asking, "What happened?"

"Training exercise."

"Oh. Wow."

Kathryn pondered that as they walked through the wide church foyer and into the sanctuary. Perhaps half-full, with the congregants gathered near the front of the space, the long, bright hall with its pale woods and white, padded pews felt foreign to Kathryn. The last time she'd been here, the room had been dark and shadowy, making it much easier to slip in unnoticed. As they moved toward the front of the sanctuary, a tall, handsome, solidly built man with dark, curly hair stood and started up the aisle to greet them, a smile on his face. Jake got up and followed along behind him.

"You made it."

"Kathryn was kind enough to come with me. Kathryn, this is my husband, Wyatt."

Wyatt Smith put out his big hand and gave Kathryn's a hearty shake. Like Jake, Wyatt had dark brown eyes and the shadow of a heavy beard on his square jaw and chin.

"Nice to meet you, Kathryn."

Tina looked to Jake then smiled and said, "She'll do."

Before Kathryn could ponder that statement, the Billings sisters rushed up to greet Kathryn with exuberant hugs.

"It's so good to see you!"

"KKay! How marvelous you look!"

Ann Billings swept a hand across the ends of Kathryn's hair. "You used to have the longest, thickest ponytail I've ever seen."

"All the boys called you Rapunzel," Meri said, laughing.

"I remember," Kathryn murmured, overwhelmed by the greeting.

The pastor entered through a door at the rear of the auditorium just then, and the piano started playing. Wyatt urged the women forward. "Better sit."

Jake held out a hand. Kathryn nodded, smiling weakly at the Billings sisters, and quickly entered the pew. Jake followed, with Tina and Wyatt bringing up the rear.

"KKay?" Jake murmured into her ear. She crossed her arms to quell the shiver that rushed over her skin.

"An old nickname," she whispered. "My middle name is Kay."

"Ah."

She sat down next to a big, muscle-bound man with sleek black hair and the dark Smith eyes and beard shadow. He nodded at her.

"My baby brother, Ryder," Jake said softly. He

placed a hand on her arm, saying to his brother, "Kathryn Stepp."

At Jake's touch, Kathryn again fought a shiver.

Ryder Smith smiled. "Hi."

"Hello."

Someone passed Ryder several papers then. He handed one to Kathryn and the rest to Jake, who passed them on. Glancing down, she saw a list of names and prayer requests. She'd requested prayers for her mother while Mia had languished in the hospital in Oklahoma City all those years ago. Would it have made a difference if she'd come to pray in person?

After the music, the pastor said a few words then prayed not only for those on the printed list but also for those who turned in request cards that evening. After the pastor, others began to pray aloud. Kathryn kept her head down, but every second she felt Jake's warm presence at her elbow. Again, she wondered if she'd offended him earlier by initially refusing to attend this meeting. She should've explained how uncomfortable big groups of strangers made her.

As the service came to a close, she glanced around her while waiting to exit the pew. She didn't know the current pastor, but to her surprise she knew quite a few of those present.

Tina was already at the door at the back of the sanctuary before Kathryn made it out to the aisle. Slipping around Jake, Kathryn quickly followed the other woman.

The Billings sisters waylaid her again in the foyer, chatting about the changes in their lives. Both had married and borne children. Their husbands soon joined them, little ones in tow. Kathryn looked on with sharp, silent envy. Meri commented on the bag that Kathryn carried, but before Kathryn could reply, something hit her from the side so hard that she stumbled. Out of nowhere, Jake steadied her, his hands at her shoulders.

"Frankie!" he scolded. "You nearly bowled her over."

Kathryn felt the boy's arms hugging her even as she looked down.

"I sorwy," he said, his eyes huge in his little face.

Smiling, Kathryn smoothed his dark, shaggy hair. "No harm done. Hello again."

He grinned at her. "Hello."

"KKay has an admirer," Meri observed, chuckling.

Frankie's brow wrinkled. "KKay?"

"It's an old nickname," Kathryn told him. "Something my friends used to call me."

"KKay my fren!" Frankie announced.

Chuckling, Kathryn said, "Yes. We're friends."

Conversation continued for several more minutes. Terribly aware of Jake at her back, Kathryn struggled to pay attention, saying little. Finally, the Billings sisters and their families began to leave. Glancing around, Kathryn realized with a start that only she, Jake and Frankie remained. When had Tina left?

"Come on," Jake said, his hand against the small of her back. "We'll take you home."

Kathryn tried not to tremble at his touch or look into his eyes for fear he would see how he affected her. Instead, she simply allowed him to escort her from the building, Frankie at his side.

"What did you think of Tina?" he asked, pointing to his truck.

"She's nice. I like her."

"I talked to her about you. If you're interested, we have a place for you at Loco Man."

Shocked, Kathryn came to a halt, bleating, "Wha-a-t?"

"A job," Jake explained. "Tina's got her hands full with her son and the B and B." Stopping in his tracks, he turned to face Kathryn. Beside them, Frankie listened to the conversation with interest.

Kathryn shook her head. "B and B? As in bed-and-breakfast?"

"That's right. She's planned to turn the ranch house into a bed-and-breakfast ever since Uncle Dodd left it to her."

Kathryn shook her head again, confused. "I—I thought he left the place to you and your brothers."

"He left the *ranch* to me and my brothers. The house is Tina's. But it's all worked out for everyone. The thing is, Tina could use some help, and you seem well qualified. You cook, right?"

"Why, yes."

"And you clean."

"Of course."

"And you obviously sew and like to decorate. Tina's at the decorating stage now, and she won't rent rooms until she has the house looking like she wants it. Oh, and I might ask you to watch Frankie. I dump him on her too often. When I have to take him along with me, he misses naps and playtime."

Kathryn tried to wrap her mind around this. "You want me to cook, clean, help Tina open a bed-and-breakfast and watch your son. Is that right?"

"That about covers it."

"But why?"

"I told you. Tina needs the help. And Frankie thinks

you're great. If you can watch him at least some of the time, it'll free me up to work on your car. Seems like a win for everyone."

Kathryn tried to formulate a reply, but her mind was reeling. Had that conversation on the ride here with Tina been a kind of job interview? Did she dare work for Jake Smith and his family? She could cook and clean, no problem, but as for the rest, she just didn't know. Despite her need for income, her natural caution wouldn't allow her to accept without thinking through this offer.

They reached the truck. Jake picked up Frankie and settled him into his seat while Kathryn let herself into the cab. Suddenly so burdened with concern that she felt on the verge of tears, Kathryn couldn't speak. In the charged atmosphere, even Frankie remained silent on the drive to her house. She just kept wondering how this had happened.

She'd liked her job. All three of her clients were sweet, harmless, elderly folk, and she knew she'd made positive differences in their lives. What did she know about children? As adorable as Frankie was, she had no experience with little ones, boys especially. And the idea of seeing Jake on a daily basis made her insides quake.

The man rattled her in ways she couldn't even describe. He'd hit her life with all the force of a whirlwind, a tall, dark, handsome whirlwind that somehow threatened to blow her careful, tidy existence to pieces. Everything familiar and comfortable in her life had disappeared since she'd met him.

Everything but her home. She still had that. For now.

Without income, she'd never be able to fix her car, let alone buy out her father.

When Jake and Frankie dropped her off at home, Jake said, "Just think about it."

Nodding, she let herself out of the truck and trudged inside to consider her options. She made a list of all the businesses in town within walking distance, but she already knew that those employed locally tended to hang on to their jobs. Calling other home care companies in the area would do no good. They'd all require proof of transportation, just as her last employer had. So it was sit at home for weeks without pay until Jake Smith got her old car running, and then hope she could get hired on with the agency again. Or accept his job offer. Seemed odd to let him pay her so she could afford to pay him for fixing her car, but she didn't see any other choice.

Despite her emotional exhaustion, she slept little that night and rose early the next morning to prepare herself to accept the job at Loco Man Ranch. With no idea when Jake—or Tina—might reach out to her again, she made a second cup of coffee and carried it out to the porch where she sat and waited, long enough that she finally resorted to prayer.

Lord, can't anything ever be easy? Can't You help? Are You even there? What if Jake's thought better of hiring me? What if I never get my car running and lose my house? I don't understand what's happening. I'm afraid.

She was so tired of being afraid.

With the temperature climbing to an uncomfortable level, she decided to go inside, but before she could get up, she heard the sound of tires on pavement and looked around to see a familiar olive-green truck turning into her drive. Correction, *army* green. So great was her relief that she feared collapsing if she tried to stand, and that kept her in her seat as Jake got out and came to her. Without a word, he crouched in front of her and pushed back the brim of his hat before removing his sunshades. Offering her a swift smile, he balanced his forearms atop his knees.

"You really should give me your phone number," she said crisply, foregoing a greeting and keeping her gaze on his chin. The man was just too handsome.

As if he knew exactly what she was thinking, he dropped his head. She suspected that he was hiding a grin, but when he looked up, he appeared perfectly composed.

"I can do that. We'll need yours, of course. Meanwhile, Tina would like for you to join us for lunch. She'll show you around the house and give you a feel for what needs doing."

Kathryn pulled in a deep breath, ignoring the way her heart sped up when his deep brown eyes met her gaze. "You should understand two things. One, I know nothing about children. Two, as soon as you get my car running again, I'll find a real job."

"You'll do fine with the kids," he said. "You're careful and protective. Besides, in case of an emergency, there are four other adults around the place. And this *is* a real job."

"This is pity," Kathryn scoffed softly, dropping her gaze, "however well intended."

"No, no, no. Tina really needs the help. The duties are many and varied. Once the B and B opens, I suspect she'll even want you to help with the guests."

That surprised Kathryn. Didn't he see how uncomfortable she was dealing with strangers? "Oh, I'm not sure I'm cut out for that."

"How will you know if you don't try?" he cajoled gently. "You might surprise yourself. Anyone who can do what you did for your mother ought to be able to manage just about anything."

Obviously, Tina had reported their conversation to him. Kathryn found, to her surprise, that she didn't much mind, especially given the sound of respect in his voice.

"We'll see."

"Then you'll take the job?"

"Yes. And thank you."

"No need for that." He pushed up to a standing position and slid his glasses back into place before tugging down the brim of his hat. "We need the help. You need the job. It's that simple."

It might be that simple for him, but Kathryn wasn't so sure about her own part in this. Oh, why did he have to be so handsome and generous? She rose and squared her shoulders, preparing for an uncomfortable day.

Eventually, she told herself, she'd lose this strange, hopeless attraction. Meanwhile, she'd have income. Then, once her car was repaired, she could put as much distance as necessary between herself and Jacoby Smith.

Please, God, she prayed. *Let it be soon.*

Hopefully before she made a complete fool of herself.

Chapter Four

As Jake walked her up the steps to the back door, Kathryn could hear Tina admonishing someone.

"I told you to get that off the table."

"Aww, Mo-o-m," came the whining reply. "We're still playing."

Frankie's little voice echoed the complaint. "We still playin'."

Jake reached around Kathryn and shoved open the door, hurrying her inside and following, right at her back.

"Francis Jacoby Smith," he barked, "apologize to your aunt Tina this minute."

Startled, Frankie paused, his hand on a tiny bright red car that he was pushing through a jumble of small toys on the terra-cotta tile tabletop. His eyes big and bright, Frankie looked to his aunt.

"I sorwy, Aunt Tina."

Tyler also apologized, bowing his strawberry blond head. "Sorry, Mom."

"Thank you, boys. Just clear away the toys, please."

Tyler got up and grabbed a plastic tub, while Frankie,

beaming now, waved at Kathryn and called out, "Hi, KKay!"

She returned his smile. "Hello, Frankie."

The boys raked the toys off the table into the tub.

"Now upstairs with you two until lunch is ready," Tina ordered. "March."

Frankie got down from his chair, and the two boys ran toward the front of the house, jostling the tub between them. Tina turned to smile at Kathryn.

"Welcome to Loco Man."

A pot simmering on the stove punctuated that statement by beginning to boil over. Tina rushed to turn down the burner before checking the contents. Kathryn ventured closer, recognizing the black-eyed peas and ham cooking in the pot. What captured her attention, however, was the stove.

"I've never seen anything like your range."

"That's because they don't make them like this anymore," Tina told her proudly. "Six burners, three ovens and storage. Our grandmothers sure knew how to do it, didn't they?"

"But it looks brand-new," Kathryn said in surprise.

Tina waved a potholder at Jake. "You can thank him for that."

Jake chuckled. "Now, if I could just cook, I'd be of some real help around here."

"I can cook," Kathryn said quickly. "I like to cook."

Tina smiled. "In that case, mind breading some okra? I never seem to get it right. I just wind up fouling my frying oil."

"No problem," Kathryn said, aware that she was likely being evaluated and hoping her voice didn't waver too much.

Tina opened a drawer and took out an apron, passing it to Kathryn. "I'm going to watch you do it so I'll know how."

Kathryn's hands shook at first, but she'd worked in enough strange kitchens under watchful eyes to manage. Tina had already poured oil into a large skillet and washed and cut the okra pods into bite-size pieces. Now she heated the oil as Kathryn worked.

"So it's three-fourths flour and a quarter cornmeal," Tina noted a few minutes later as she dropped the okra into the frying pan.

More relaxed now, Kathryn shyly gave her a piece of advice. "The key to breading just about anything is to dust it with flour *before* dredging it in the egg. Then you can coat it evenly with your breading. One of my elderly clients clued me in."

"There you are," Tina quipped. "The older generation does know best."

They both laughed. Only when she turned did Kathryn realize that Jake was leaning against the table, watching. That both pleased and unnerved her. She found her feelings toward him to be terribly confusing. As a girl, she'd liked certain boys and had even harbored a few fantasies, but she'd never really been attracted to anyone. Then again, she'd never before known a man like Jake. As if sensing her discomfort, he lurched to his feet.

"Think I'll check on the boys."

Tina bowed her head, a small smile curving her lush lips. Kathryn felt plain and spare next to Tina, but at least she wasn't uncomfortable around this particular Smith. In fact, she'd meant it when she'd told Jake that she liked Tina.

At Tina's direction, Kathryn helped prepare the remainder of the meal. When Wyatt came in to kiss his wife and clean up, Kathryn busied herself setting the table. Ryder arrived just moments later, brushing white dust from his shoulders and his hair.

"That's usually my job," he said to Kathryn, grinning. "Does this mean I'm off kitchen detail permanently?"

"Oh, I don't know about that," Kathryn murmured hesitantly, glancing at Tina, who rolled her eyes at Ryder.

"Leave the woman alone. She's cooked half your meal. Now you're asking her to take over your measly kitchen chores."

Ryder just grinned and went to the refrigerator for a huge pitcher of iced tea. "If she can hang drywall, I'll gladly trade my job for hers."

"As a cook, your drywall-hanging skills are exceptional," Tina quipped dryly.

Chuckling, Wyatt said to Kathryn, "Truth is, Tina's been doing just about everything around here on her own, and it's held up her plans for the B and B."

"I hope I can be of help," Kathryn remarked uncertainly.

"Can't imagine you won't," Jake said, ushering Frankie and Tyler back into the room. "We're looking forward to that fried okra."

Blushing, Kathryn helped get the meal on the table then sat in the chair Tina pointed out to her. Placed between Frankie and Jake, Kathryn felt the latter at her back as he helped slide the heavy wrought-iron chair under the table. The moment the chair was in place, Frankie leaned over and wrapped his arms around her neck, squeezing mightily, his booster seat bringing him almost to her height. He then beamed at Tyler, exclaiming, "My KKay!"

Tyler looked confused, but all the adults started laughing—except Kathryn.

Jake explained. "Frankie is famous for assigning ownership of the people in his life. Not long ago he 'gave' Wyatt to Tyler for a father."

"Worked, too, didn't it?" Wyatt teased, winking at Frankie and mussing Tyler's reddish blond hair. Tyler beamed. Clearly he was pleased with Wyatt Smith as a stepfather.

Finally, they were all gathered at the long, rectangular table. To Kathryn's shock, Jake reached for her hand. Only when Frankie tapped her on the arm and held out his hand for her to take did she understand that everyone was linking hands around the table.

"We do dis," Frankie instructed, bowing his head.

Kathryn obediently bowed her head, biting her lips to hide a smile. Jake squeezed her hand. She cut a glance at him from the corner of her eye, but he sat like stone next to her. She wondered if she'd imagined that squeeze.

Wyatt said, "Jake, why don't you bless our meal?"

Jake cleared his throat and began to pray. "Lord God, we thank You and praise You for Your many blessings and Your boundless generosity. Every time we have need, You provide. Thank you for this food and especially for those who prepared it. Amen."

He released her hand as if it were a hot potato. Quietly glancing around the table, Kathryn tried to concentrate on the fact that he'd just given thanks for her, in an oblique, impersonal fashion. Letting her gaze move from face to face, she told herself that it didn't matter if he felt uncomfortable holding her hand. These were good, kind people, and she was here to work, nothing more. To work and, apparently, to pray.

Come to think of it, she'd prayed earlier that day in sheer desperation, and now here she sat, employed and welcome, her car being repaired. Was that not God meeting her needs? It occurred to her that she had also prayed that morning when her car had broken down, and along had come Jacoby Smith. Why would any man go to such extremes to help someone he didn't even know? Her prayers hadn't even been good prayers, as much complaint as entreaty, but she couldn't deny that her needs were being met.

Ashamed for thinking that God might have abandoned her, she listened to the easy banter of those around her and filled her plate as the dishes were passed to her. Before long, she recognized an unusual feeling rising within her.

It was gratitude. And just a whisper of sweet, sweet hope.

"This is so nice," Kathryn said, taking in the beautifully tiled bathroom. "I love the antique look of the vanity. Forest green would really make the most of all this bright white tile. I confess I'm partial to greens."

"Ooh, that would be gorgeous."

Kathryn swept a finger over the green-and-tan motif pressed into the accent tile. "I'm thinking natural wicker for smaller accents."

"Brilliant!" Tina exclaimed. "I can actually see it all coming together now."

A small hand tugged on hers. "KKay, see my room."

Tyler had gone to play, but Frankie had been following them from room to room, watching and listening, sometimes beetle-browed.

Smiling down at the boy, Kathryn nodded. "Okay. Show me."

Obviously delighted, he tugged her out of the bathroom and along the hallway to his small room. The walls had been painted a buttery gold. The furnishings were all constructed of gleaming golden oak. A practical rug in a warm, medium brown lay beside the narrow bed. Short curtains of the same color flanked the single window where several colorful light catchers had been hung. Kathryn watched, smiling, as he opened his closet door to reveal neat shelves stocked with toys and a few articles of clothing hanging from a short rod. A series of stuffed animals, all dogs except for a teddy bear and a rabbit, lined the top of his tall dresser.

"What a great room," she enthused, remembering his desire for a real dog. "You know what it needs?"

Staring up raptly into her face, he shook his head.

"Puppies."

"Puppies!" Frankie cheered, hopping up and down and clapping his hands.

"I have a stencil," she said to Tina, holding up her hands to demonstrate its size, about one-by-three feet. "Would you mind if I painted some puppies on the walls?"

"What a fun idea," Tina said. "I don't mind, and I'm sure Jake won't, either."

Kathryn bit her lips. She hadn't even thought of consulting Jake. She would remember to do so in the future.

"Now," Tina said, "about the master bedroom…"

Kathryn followed Tina downstairs, leaving Frankie in Tyler's room, gushing about puppies. After several minutes in the master bedroom, Kathryn said, "I think you need a contrasting print in here, but the colors need to be exact. I have some swatch books I can bring over for you to look at."

Tina cocked her head, studying Kathryn. "I get the feeling that you intend to make a lot of the items we've talked about. Jake says you made everything in your house."

Worried that Jake had misrepresented her qualifications, Kathryn shook her head. "I may have said that, but I didn't mean it literally. It's not like I built the furniture or anything."

"You just upholstered and slipcovered it all," Tina surmised with a grin. "And apparently, you made a remarkable rug."

"It's just an oval rug for the coffee table to sit on."

Laughing, Tina shook her head. "You have no idea how talented you are, do you?"

Both pleased and mortified, Kathryn bit her lips and said nothing.

"I wish I had a sewing machine here for you to use."

More excited than she wanted Tina to know, Kathryn quickly offered to bring over her machine. "It's old but portable and makes a fine stitch."

"That's a wonderful idea. Bring anything you like. You can set up in the laundry room."

"Perfect. There's plenty of space in there, and the counter is just the right height. Plus, I saw several electrical outlets."

"We'll have to move some things so you can get a

chair under the counter, but that shouldn't be a problem."

"I don't want to be a bother."

"A bother? Pfft. I already know you're going to be a huge asset."

Thrilled, Kathryn dipped her head and bit her lips. Tina let her know that she was ready to move on by pointing toward the door. They walked out into the hallway and turned toward the kitchen, where they found Jake and Wyatt nursing glasses of iced tea and talking quietly.

"Once the parts start coming in, you can split your days," Wyatt was saying. "Ryder will help."

"You need him to finish up the bunkhouse and take care of the horses," Jake said.

"He can split his days, too. Besides, the bunkhouse can wait. He doesn't care that the walls aren't painted yet or whether the baseboards are down. I suggest the two of you work on the garage in the cool of the mornings and save the afternoons for—"

Jake waved a hand, cutting him off midsentence. He nodded at Kathryn and Tina, calling Wyatt's attention to them. Wyatt got up and pulled out a chair for Tina. At the same time, Jake stood and pulled out a chair next to him for Kathryn. The women sat, and Tina leaned forward to address Jake.

"You were so right about her." Tina straightened, looked at her husband and gushed, "Wait until you see what we have planned. Thanks to Kathryn, I've finally got a real vision for this place."

"Oh, no," Kathryn said quickly. "You've established the style very well. I've just suggested some decoration."

"It's going to be beautiful," Tina told Wyatt.

"You mean it isn't already? All I see is beautiful. No, wait. That's my wife."

Laughing, Tina half rose and kissed him, leaning on her forearms. Jake glanced at Kathryn, pushed back his chair and rose.

"I think that's my cue to leave."

"Why don't you take Kathryn home now?" Tina said. "I think I picked her brain clean this afternoon. She's probably ready to kick back for a while."

"But shouldn't I start dinner?" Kathryn asked anxiously.

Tina patted her hands on the tabletop. "Nope. I've already planned to pull a casserole out of the freezer. Just needs heating up. You're welcome to stay and eat, but you've done enough for one day."

"Guess I'll see you tomorrow then." Kathryn stood as Jake pulled out her chair. "What time should I be here?"

Tina considered. "We'll discuss lunch and dinner tomorrow. I'll need you here for cleanup after the evening meal, so say…about ten? Half past maybe."

Kathryn looked to Jake. He was her only transportation, after all.

"Ten thirty it is." He nodded at Kathryn. "I'll be there a quarter after."

Tina got up and slipped around the table to quickly hug Kathryn. "I think working with you is going to be fun." To Jake she said, "We'll look after Frankie until you get back."

"I appreciate that."

"Have a good evening."

Nodding, Kathryn let Jake steer her toward the back

door, his hand resting against the small of her back. It was a meaningless gesture, she knew, but she was keenly aware of that gentle hand as they moved together out the door, down the steps and along the concrete pad of what Wyatt, according to Tina, intended to be a massive carport. Kathryn climbed up into the cab of Jake's pickup truck, surveying the house as Jake walked around and got in behind the steering wheel.

The big old house had been freshly painted the color of aged parchment and trimmed in a medium grayish brown that looked good with the shiny metal roof. Kathryn thought the house needed decorative shutters in that same brown and green window boxes filled with flowers. Painting the rocking chairs on the porch and adding a pair of planters would dress up the place, too.

"So, you and Tina settle all the particulars?" Jake asked, interrupting her reverie.

Kathryn nodded, then shook her head. "Just about. Tina didn't mention salary."

"Didn't she?" Jake started the engine and checked his mirrors before backing out the truck. "Well, we discussed it. She must've assumed I'd told you." He shifted the transmission into Drive and headed the truck toward the highway. "How does this sound?" Just before he turned the truck onto the pavement, he named an hourly figure that made Kathryn gasp.

"Are you sure? That's almost twice what I made in my last job."

"You'll be doing more than you were in that job," he pointed out casually.

Kathryn bit her lips for a moment, thinking. "I suppose that's true." She beat down tears of relief, struggling to remain impassive. "Maybe I can afford to fix the car, after all. Doesn't seem right, though, to pay you for fixing my car with money you're paying me."

"Believe me, no one's complaining about this arrangement. Least of all Frankie."

Frankie. Struck by the thought that she should have taken her leave of the boy, Kathryn began apologizing. "He doesn't know I've gone. I didn't think to say goodbye. Maybe we should go back so I can."

"Oh, man." Jake chuckled. "You're going to spoil my kid rotten, aren't you?"

"No. I—I just don't want him to think I'm abandoning him."

"That's the last thing I worry about. You didn't abandon your mom when most girls your age would have."

Kathryn smiled, but then she winced. "In a way, though, I did abandon my former clients."

"That wasn't your fault. You were tired after your car broke down. That's not abandonment by any stretch of the imagination."

Warmed by his defense of her, she fought a smile. "They depended on me. They won't know the new helper, but I'll try to keep in touch with them. It's the least I can do. So is saying goodbye to Frankie."

"When Frankie notices you're gone, everyone will tell him that you'll be back in the morning. Wish I could say that about the puppy he's expecting."

Kathryn snapped her fingers. "That reminds me. Is it okay with you if I stencil puppies on the walls of Frankie's room? I sort of promised him."

"Yep," Jake said. "Spoiled rotten." He flashed her a quick smile. "I don't mind at all."

In the silence that followed, Kathryn closed her eyes

and mentally thanked God. *Now if You can just do something about my house…*

Maybe her father would accept monthly payments. She'd figure out what she could afford to pay with this new job and make him an offer. But what if this job didn't last? Only this morning she'd told herself this job was temporary, and now she was worried it wouldn't last. What foolishness. If the Smiths weren't pleased with her or she couldn't get over this silly infatuation with Jake, she'd go back to home healthcare. Or maybe she'd babysit full-time.

That brought up another concern. She jerked her eyes open to see that they were almost to her house.

"We didn't discuss my duties concerning Frankie."

Jake turned the truck into her drive and brought it to a stop. He rubbed a forefinger over his eyebrow. "Well, if you can just keep an eye on him. Maybe get him down for his nap when I'm not around. Manage his snacks." He shook his head, smiling. "That boy can eat his weight in sweets, so keep those to a minimum." He spread his hands. "You know, just sort of step in when I'm not around."

"I can do that. With Tyler, too, if needed."

Nodding, Jake said, "I'll be sure to let Tina know."

"Okay then." Kathryn released her seat belt and opened her door, but then she paused to meet his gaze. She'd thanked God, but Jake deserved her gratitude, too. "Thank you, Jake. For everything. I don't know what I'd have done if you hadn't stopped to help."

Shrugging, he said, "Seems to me it's all working out for the best."

"I hope so. From the bottom of my heart, thank you."

Shifting in his seat, he lifted his hands and gripped the steering wheel, his jaw hardening. Taking that to mean he was ready to get home, she slipped out onto the ground.

"See you tomorrow."

"A quarter after ten," he confirmed, his voice oddly strangled.

She hurried to the porch, paused to wave and let herself into the house. Only after she closed the door did he back out the truck and drive away. For the first time since her old car had begun to lurch and sputter on the way to Sandy's house, she wasn't worried. Well, not too much. Her father's claim on the house still had to be settled. But first things first. Once her car was repaired, she'd contact her father and try to work out something. Meanwhile, things were looking up.

She had a job. And maybe friends, too.

Strangely, despite the breakdown of her car, that was more than she'd had in a long time.

Chapter Five

Had he lost what remained of his tiny mind?

Horrified with himself, Jake could barely manage not to squeal his tires on the pavement of Kathryn's street.

He'd very nearly kissed the woman! She'd looked at him all soft-eyed and trusting, and he'd instantly, desperately wanted to kiss her. Only by throttling the steering wheel had he managed not to haul her into his arms and show her that he was less Good Samaritan than interested male.

And that salary! What had possessed him to name such a figure? The rest of the family would think he was crazy. Maybe he was. God knew he couldn't afford to burn through his money before the garage was up and running, but he was obligated now. He was appalled to realize that he might have been acting out of unrecognized attraction all along.

Kathryn Kay Stepp was as prickly as a wounded porcupine, but the first time she showed the slightest inclination to fold her spines, he'd wanted to leap at her and drag her into his arms. She'd just barely relaxed her guard around him, and he'd come within a heartbeat of pushing their feeble, casual relationship to a new—and probably fatal—level.

Idiot.

Kathryn was right to distrust him, and that upset him as much as the thought of Jolene. Not even two years since his wife's death, and he was jumping at the first woman he'd come across in this state. And she was nothing at all like Jolene!

That alone felt like a kind of betrayal. It was as if he'd stumbled into some ugly bog of emotions, and before he knew what was happening, he'd blown right past the ranch. He didn't begin to calm until he drew near the place where he'd first seen Kathryn's car broken down beside the road. A few hundred yards beyond the spot, he finally slowed to a stop and ran a hand over his face.

"Lord, how do I get myself back on solid ground?" he asked.

He didn't know why she affected him so. She was timid and guarded and generally uncommunicative, while Jolene had been the opposite in every way. Yet Kathryn was also courageous, dedicated, capable, lovely...

Okay, he needed to keep his distance, at least until this fascination wore off. He didn't have the time or money for a relationship right now. He'd do well to get the garage operational and repair her car before he exhausted his funds.

Frowning at himself, he turned the truck around and headed back to the house. As he brought the vehicle to a stop in its customary spot, he prepared himself for the scrutiny of his brother and sister-in-law. Maybe his envy of those two had as much to do with his attraction to Kathryn as anything else. If so, it would play itself out soon enough.

Meanwhile, he'd keep as much distance between himself and Kathryn Stepp as the situation allowed and clamp down on his personal expenses so he could afford to pay her the difference between what he'd promised and what he, Wyatt and Tina had agreed to. Remembering the surprise and delight in Kathryn's big green eyes when he'd told her what her pay would be, he smiled. Then he sternly told himself to cut it out.

He could manage this, and it wouldn't be for long. Kathryn had as good as told him that she would be looking for another job as soon as possible. Relieved, he congratulated himself on reasoning through the situation. When he walked into the house, he felt calm and unconcerned.

Tina's casserole heated in the oven, filling the kitchen with appetizing aromas. He found Wyatt and Tina in the den, snuggled up on the couch watching cable news. Both looked at him.

Wyatt asked, "Get Kathryn home okay?"

"Sure."

"Tina's been talking nonstop about Kathryn's ideas for decorating the house."

Jake tried very hard not to acknowledge a swell of pride. He had no business taking pride in her talents. "That's good."

"Kind of funny," Wyatt remarked, "such a plain woman being such a whiz at decorating."

Both Jake and Tina spoke at the same time. "She's not plain!"

"She just hides her light under a basket," Tina

added. "Get her into some fashionable clothes, shape up her hair a bit, give her a little confidence, she could be a knockout."

"If you say so," Wyatt muttered.

Jake wanted to growl at his brother. What nonsense. Kathryn, plain? Hardly. And she was just fine as she was. Wyatt laid his head back on the sofa and smiled meaningfully. Jake didn't even want to consider what that smile meant, but it reaffirmed his decision to keep his distance from their new employee. Jake changed the subject.

"Where's Frankie?"

"Upstairs playing," Wyatt said. "When he realized you and Kathryn were gone, he asked for his pony. I took him out and let him pet the pony in its stall." Wyatt tossed Jake a pointed look. "He promised the horse they'd go riding real soon."

"Yeah, I've got to do something about that." One more drain on his time. Still, his son needed instruction. The problem was, he didn't know what to do. "Nothing Uncle Dodd taught us about horses has settled down that critter or helped Frankie keep control of it."

"Maybe we ought to talk to Stark about it," Wyatt suggested. He and the busy veterinarian had become fast friends. "According to Rex, the man knows more about horses than anyone around." Rex Billings was a local rancher and attorney, and Stark Burns was his brother-in-law.

"Good to know," Jake replied. "I'll go check on Frankie now."

Surprised to find his son playing in his own room, Jake took a seat on the narrow bed, smiling.

"What's up? You and Tyler have a little falling-out maybe?"

Frankie just looked at him. "Ty'er room cars. KKay gettin' puppies on my wall!"

"I know. She told me. Won't that be fun?" Apparently to Frankie, just the promise of puppies was more fun than Tyler's car-themed room. Nodding, Frankie got up, came over and crawled into Jake's lap.

"Where KKay?"

"I took her home, but she'll be back in the morning."

"S'let go her."

"No, we can't go to her. She has other things to do tonight."

Frankie huffed and laid his head on Jake's chest. What a pair they were, both wrapped up in a woman they barely knew.

"Hey, want to watch some TV in Dad's room? We have some time before dinner."

Frankie nodded, so Jake stood with the boy in his arms and carried him into his bedroom. He wondered if Tina had shown this drab, utilitarian room to Kathryn, and if so, what her suggestions might have been. Mentally closing off that thought, he dropped Frankie onto the bed and smiled as Frankie bounced, laughing. Jake vaulted over him, jostling the mattress again just to make his son laugh.

They settled onto the pillows. Picking up the remote control on his bedside table, Jake aimed it at the flat-screen TV on the wall and pressed the On switch. After quickly finding Frankie's preferred channel, Jake tossed aside the remote and folded his arms behind his head, grinning as Frankie copied the action.

They watched the kid's program until Tina called

them down to dinner a few minutes later. Baths, books and bedtime followed. As Jake drew the curtains over Frankie's bedroom window—summer days in Oklahoma were long and bright—he felt his own weariness. He shouldn't be so tired. He'd worked on Kathryn's car for a few hours that morning, but he hadn't even gotten to the difficult part yet. So far it had been about loosening and disconnecting stuff under the hood so he could get to the motor mounts. He hadn't even made it over to the shop site today, and if he was going to get up early enough to get anything done over there, he'd have to turn in early.

Settling in to sleep, he closed his eyes. And saw Kathryn gazing at him with that soft, pleased look on her face.

After tossing and turning for what felt like hours, he finally drifted off, only to wake groggy and stiff before dawn the next morning, having slept too heavily for too short a time. He dressed and quietly left the house.

When he arrived at the shop site mere minutes later, he found Ryder already there, mixing mortar for the cement blocks with which they were building walls. Wyatt must have spoken to him about helping out, because Jake had not. Smiling, he clapped Ryder on the shoulder.

"Thanks, man."

"Let's get to it," Ryder said, slapping mortar onto the top of the last row of cement blocks that Jake had laid.

Working together, they put up almost an entire row of blocks before Jake's phone told him it was time to knock off so he could make it to Kathryn's at the specified time. He hated to leave the row unfinished, but Kathryn, Tina and Frankie were depending on him.

"Time to grab some breakfast."

Ryder didn't argue. Back at the house, they strode into the kitchen together and hung their hats on two of several pegs on the wall. Ryder headed to the bathroom in the back hall to wash up, but Jake decided a quick shower was in order.

He stopped by Frankie's room ten minutes later to find it empty. As soon as he stepped into the kitchen, Frankie waved his fork in the air, yelling, "KKay comin'!"

Obviously, his weren't the only thoughts constantly hijacked by Kathryn. "She'll be here soon, so you better finish up there."

Frankie began wolfing down his breakfast. Jake, on the other hand, had to make himself eat. He often lost his appetite in moments of stress. He tried not to think about all he had to do that day, but that just gave him space to think about Kathryn. Did she know he had almost kissed her? He prayed not.

The boys finished eating and ran upstairs to dress for the day. Ryder carried his plate to the counter and headed out to care for the horses. Wyatt announced that he was going over to see a bull that Stark was holding for the owner.

In a sense, the veterinarian and his family were the Smiths' closest neighbors. Their place was across the road, loosely referred to as a highway by the locals, and a mile or less east, past Stuart Westhaven's farm supply store and grain silos. All three establishments— the Loco Man compound, the grain yard and the Burns home and veterinary practice—were located well outside the city limits.

"I'll ask Stark what we should do about that pony," Wyatt commented, taking his hat from a hook by the door.

Irritated that Wyatt seemed to think he was the ultimate authority where Frankie was concerned, Jake shook his head. Frankie was *his* kid, and *he* would take care of this issue. "I'll stop by there on my way to pick up Kathryn."

"Suit yourself." Wyatt kissed Tina, put on his hat and left.

"I should tell you that Kathryn is bringing her portable sewing machine today," Tina said. "I expect there will probably be some other things, sewing notions at least. Oh, and we'll need to move the boxes we've stashed under the counter in the laundry room." She started to turn away but stopped. "A chair. We'll have to find a decent chair for her."

"My old desk chair is out in the barn," Jake said. "It should fit nicely under the counter. I'll haul those boxes out there and bring the chair in."

"Excellent."

He quickly toted several boxes from under the laundry room counter to the barn then found the chair and hauled it inside. Frankie and Tyler waited for him in the kitchen.

"We get KKay," Frankie insisted happily.

Remembering what Tina had said about Kathryn bringing her sewing machine, Jake realized that the boys could easily get underfoot. Strangely relieved to have a reason to deny them, Jake shook his head. He told himself it was because he didn't have time to add

Tyler's car seat to Frankie's in his truck, but he worried that he might enjoy those moments when he had Kathryn to himself a little too much. Imagine how he'd feel if the woman liked him. What then?

For a moment, everything about the current situation weighed on Jake. What if he ran out of money before he got the garage open? What if the business he expected never materialized so the garage failed? Maybe he and Frankie would be better off back in Houston. He could get a job there. He wouldn't have to worry about building his own shop, running out of money or failing at business, and Kathryn Stepp would be just an interesting memory. But he and Frankie would be living far away from their only family, and Jake had already given up his military career to raise his son with the uncles he adored. They'd added stability to Frankie's life when Jake and Jolene hadn't been able to do so themselves.

He felt a pang of guilt at resenting Wyatt's penchant for assuming responsibility for Frankie. That was just Wyatt, and Jake had no doubt that if anything ever happened to him, Wyatt and Ryder would step in to raise Frankie without a heartbeat's hesitation. He couldn't take Frankie away from them. No, he had to see this plan through, no matter what.

"Sorry, son. I'm going to be moving some things for KKay," Jake said. "You boys stay here out of harm's way. I'll be back soon. With KKay." Frankie's bottom lip plumped, but Tyler slid an arm across Frankie's shoulders and suggested they go play with his dog, Tipper. Jake let Tina know that the boys had gone outside and set off for Kathryn's.

On the way, he impulsively decided to stop at the

Burns place. Maybe he could catch Wyatt and Stark and include Wyatt in the conversation about Frankie's pony. The clinic was closed up tight, though, and Wyatt's truck was nowhere to be seen. A bull stood by itself in the pen out back. Jake drove around to the house, a large, modern brick affair that completely dwarfed the small clapboard clinic. Meredith, Stark's wife, said that Wyatt and Stark had gone over to speak to the owner of the bull Wyatt was considering.

"They won't be long. You're welcome to come in and wait."

"Thanks, but I have to go pick up Kathryn."

Meredith Billings Burns smiled and tilted her head. "Do you mind if I ask how you met Kathryn? She's been the next thing to a hermit for years. After her mom died, several of her old friends reached out to her, invited her to dinner, things like that. She was polite, but she refused, so we backed off. Then suddenly I see her at church with you and your family."

"Church was Tina's doing," Jake said, still smarting because Kathryn had refused to accompany him to the midweek service. "All I did was stop and help her when her car broke down beside the road."

Meredith considered that. "Interesting. I'd expect to have a difficult time getting her to let me help her, and I've known her since kindergarten."

"Huh. Well, the thing is, I'm a mechanic, so—"

"Really? We could use a good mechanic around here."

"That's why I'm building a shop. Already poured the foundation and started putting up the walls."

"So that's what's going on. We saw the cement

mixer come by but just assumed the driver was lost. Who's your builder? Lyons and Son?"

"No. Lyons is good, but my brother and I are doing most of the work ourselves. Takes longer, but it's cheaper, and I'm hoping not to borrow any money."

"Sensible."

"Hope so. Well, Kathryn's expecting me, and I'm late." He started to leave then thought better of it. "She's working for us now. Working for Tina, I mean. That's why I'm picking her up. It's not…her car's not running."

"Ah. Well, I'm just happy to know that she's around people her own age for a change. It's been years, you know, ten at least."

"More like eleven or twelve," he corrected automatically. Meredith's smile made him wish he'd kept his mouth shut. "Since her mother's accident, anyway. I don't know anything about her life before that. Or even since."

"She was well liked in school," Meri informed him, "but her shyness kept her apart somewhat. She never went to the slumber parties or football games. Then, of course, her father left her to care for her mom when she was just seventeen. I doubt she's ever even been on a date."

"I can't believe that," Jake retorted, aware as he said it that he was giving himself away. "Not that it's any of my business." He chuckled to show that what Kathryn had or had not done was of no importance to him. But he was shocked to think that Meredith might be right. No. Couldn't be. "Well, I'll stop by to speak with Stark later."

"You do that," Meri said with a smile. "He'll be opening the clinic shortly."

Jake nodded to show that he understood, waved a farewell and was standing at Kathryn's door five minutes later. He didn't have to wait long for her to answer his knock. She greeted him with the brightest smile he'd seen from her yet.

"Sorry I'm late."

"Are you late? I've been so busy I didn't notice." Sweeping an arm at the pile of boxes, bags, sewing machine and plastic tubs, she added, "I have some things to take with us." Looking over the accumulated stuff, her smile wilted. She bit her lips, as if fearing she had assembled too much. Something in him rebelled at that.

"We made space this morning." Jake rubbed his hands together. "Let's get loaded."

She brightened at once and began gathering what she could carry. "I know it's a lot, but I have whole bolts of fabric and books of swatches that I picked up when the fabric store here closed. You remember when Gladys Page had her shop downtown? Oh, no, you wouldn't. That was years ago. My mother was still in the hospital. Gladys let me have a lot of stuff for free because I helped her clear out the place. I always wondered what I'd do with some of it, and now I know. I've even got an idea for the bunkhouse." Having gathered up the smaller items, she paused. "I hope I've got something that'll work for the master bedroom. If not, we'll have to go shopping."

"I know how you women love to shop," Jake commented absently, turning to follow her with an armload of fabric in bolts. Shopping had been one of Jolene's favorite pastimes, and Tina seemed to spend more time shopping online than anything else.

Kathryn stopped in her tracks and looked over her

shoulder at him with a worried expression. "I hate it. But then since my mom's accident, I've never had any money to shop or anyone to go with me." She brightened. "I do like a good antique store, though. It'll be fun to look for things for the ranch house with Tina. We're hoping to find some wicker accessories."

She went on in that vein as they trooped out to the truck and stowed the items. Bubbling over with ideas, she talked nonstop. Jake was shocked by such a babbling, animated Kathryn, but he found this enthusiastic, happy woman breathtaking. It was a good thing he had so much to load. The impulse to hug her made him dizzy. He wondered what she'd do if he tried it. Then he realized abruptly that she might not be the only one to object.

No matter what Meredith Billings Burns said, Kathryn could well have a boyfriend—or several—for all he or anyone else knew. Every man in the whole county couldn't be blind. Besides, what did he really know about her? If she were as private as Meredith said, she could be seriously involved with none the wiser, except the guy himself. But if such a fellow existed, why wasn't *he* here helping her? Why wasn't *he* driving her around?

Could be he worked out of town, or drove a semi. Frowning, Jake silently contemplated the possibilities as Kathryn climbed up into the truck cab, still chattering.

"Oh, and I have the perfect fabric for place mats. They'll work beautifully with that terra-cotta tabletop."

Jake closed the door and walked around the front of the truck, only to realize that she was bailing out before he could even get in.

"I almost forgot to lock up!"

He watched her race into the house and return with her bag. She slung it over one shoulder, getting it out of the way while she used her key. The notion struck him that she'd probably made the bag herself. He remembered Meredith mentioning something about it as the women had chatted in the church vestibule on Wednesday.

What self-respecting man, Jake asked himself, would watch his woman do without the things that other women took for granted, like handbags and new clothes and a dependable car? He remembered what Tina had said about Kathryn's father abandoning the family after his wife's accident. With an example like that, Kathryn might be willing to accept far less from a man than a woman like her was entitled to.

Someone should show her different. Not him, though. Even if she didn't dislike him, he was in no position to provide for her. It would be all he could do to pay the wages he'd promised her, get her car running and open the garage without bankrupting himself.

He handed her up into the truck once more, resisting the urge to let himself touch her more than absolutely necessary. He couldn't help thinking, *Lord, this is not what I call solid ground. On the other hand, You've been known to help others walk on water.*

He just hoped he wasn't about to find himself in over his head.

They were halfway back to Loco Man when Kathryn suddenly remarked, "You're awful quiet."

He shifted in his seat. "Lot on my mind. First, there's Frankie's pony. That's why I was late. I tried to talk to the veterinarian about it earlier. Hopefully, he can help me figure out how to tame that contrary little beast."

"The pony, you mean," she clarified.

"Yes, the pony," Jake said, grinning. Shy and private she might be, but she couldn't help those protective instincts, not when it came to Frankie, anyway. He'd called her a worrywart that first day, but she was more of a polite Mama Bear. "I'm perfectly aware that my son is no beast. He is, however, fearless on the back of a horse, even though he's not as in control as he needs to be."

"He'll figure it out," Kathryn assured him. "You'll keep working with him, and he'll figure it out."

"Yeah. Eventually."

"So what's next?"

"Huh?"

"You said you had a lot on your mind, and first thing was Frankie and his pony. I just wondered what was next."

"Right." He waved a hand. "Well, there's the shop."

"What shop?"

"I told you I was building an auto repair shop."

"Oh. That's right. Where is it?"

"A few hundred yards from the house, fronting the road."

"Sounds convenient."

"That's the idea. We're putting up the concrete block walls now. Meanwhile, I'm buying all the stuff I'll need to get operational."

"And working on my car," she said apologetically.

He shrugged. "Ryder's helping out."

"I'm sure you'll be glad when you no longer have

to drive me everywhere. That'll be one thing off your mind."

As if, he thought, *I haven't been able to get you off my mind since I met you*.

He said, "Aw, that's no big deal. It's just a few minutes each way."

"I guess you'll need me to look after Frankie even more once your shop opens."

Now, why hadn't he thought of that? She was entirely right. "I will," he told her, hoping he didn't sound as surprised—or dismayed—as he felt. So much for temporary situations and keeping his distance.

Lord, help me, he prayed.

Why did he think this was one prayer that wouldn't be answered as he hoped?

Chapter Six

Frankie greeted Kathryn with hugs. While he towed her off to see Tyler's dog, Jake unloaded her stuff and hurried away. Afterward, despite Frankie's "help," Kathryn was able to organize and settle her sewing materials into the laundry room before Tina sent the boys upstairs to play so she and Kathryn could look through fabrics and talk decor. Frankie soon returned to usurp Kathryn's attention, however.

"My puppies," he pleaded.

Kathryn pulled out the stencil and took him upstairs to begin the process. He lay on the bed, his little chin propped on the heels of his hands, and watched as she drew a level line around three walls of the room. She taped the stencil to the wall to show Frankie where the puppies would go, but she couldn't paint without first sanding the area smooth. Before she could begin that, Tina called her downstairs to talk about lunch.

They'd barely discussed the menu when a contractor arrived to consult with Tina about the massive carport that Wyatt had planned just outside the back door. According to Tina, Wyatt wanted the door, steps and stoop covered, too. That meant connecting the roof of the carport to the house. Tina's main concern was that the carport look period appropriate and not detract from the house. While Tina and the contractor pored over architectural styles on the computer, Kathryn made lunch on her own. Tina had told her that the guys would eat almost anything but loved Mexican food in particular.

By the time Ryder came in, followed within minutes by Wyatt, Kathryn had an enormous chicken-and-rice dish on the table, along with a spinach salad, sliced melon and flour tortillas. After seeing out the contractor, Tina stood with her hands on her hips and shook her head.

"Beats the stuffing out of ham-and-cheese sandwiches." She shook a finger at Kathryn. "I need to pick your brain about the breakfast menu for the B and B."

Pleased, Kathryn said she'd look through her cookbooks. "I've got a bunch of old ones that belonged to my grandmother. There's some good stuff in them."

Tina waved a hand at the table against the far wall that she used as her personal desk. "There's the computer, too."

"I don't know much about computers. Anything, really."

"You'll get the hang of it," Tina promised, just as Jake came through the door.

"I'll do the cooking and leave the computer to you," Kathryn replied happily.

The boys clambered down the stairs and soon appeared in the kitchen. Tina swept them into the bathroom to wash up, while Kathryn went to the refrigerator for salsa and iced tea. As they all took their places around the table, Wyatt announced that he'd bought another bull and turned it into the south pasture.

"Hopefully we'll grow the herd and have a few head ready for market by this time next year."

"That's good news," Tina said, clasping his hand.

Everyone else linked hands then. Kathryn noticed that Jake held her hand loosely. Tyler was deputized to lead the prayer this time. He showed no signs of self-consciousness but kept it brief. Wyatt, Tina and Ryder chatted about their mornings as they filled plates.

Last to serve himself, Jake neither looked at anyone nor spoke. A whisper of unease filtered through Kathryn. Wyatt also seemed to sense Jake's withdrawal and tried to bring him into the conversation.

"Did you get to talk to Stark?"

"Yep."

"And did he have any ideas about what to do with that pony?"

Jake nodded, his attention fixed on his plate.

Wyatt pushed him a little. "What did Stark say?"

"He thinks we're using the wrong tack, and he had some advice on training."

"Which is?"

"We can discuss it tonight. I have to eat and get back on that car."

Kathryn's unease increased. "I—I can start paying you back for the parts next week," she told him softly. "My last paycheck from my previous employer should be in the bank by Monday." Jake responded with the barest of nods, prompting her to speak further. "A-and, of course, I'll recompense you for your work, too."

"We can discuss that later," Jake said briskly, stirring his arroz con pollo in such a fashion that she worried he found it unappetizing. She had made it on the mild side because of the boys, but the salsa should have added enough spice for him.

"As long as you know that—"

"Later," Jake snapped.

An awkward silence followed. Tina cleared her throat and launched into a description of what she and Kathryn had planned for the master bedroom.

"Sounds great," Wyatt said, smiling. "Ought to be very pretty."

"It won't be too feminine," Tina promised. Tina had been adamant about that. Some sort of silent communication sizzled between husband and wife. Kathryn looked away, a little embarrassed by the cozy, affectionate air that so often surrounded the couple.

Ryder forked up a bite of food and waved it at Kathryn. "This is really good."

Kathryn smiled and said, "Glad you're enjoying it."

Talk turned to Tina's visit with the contractor that morning. Kathryn ate in silence, casting glances around the table. All the Smith brothers were handsome men, but something about Jake drew her and had done so from the beginning, so much so that she'd felt nervous and wary around him. This morning, she'd thought they were becoming more comfortable with each other, but now he seemed to be sending off waves of…it felt like disappointment or hostility. Or maybe it was just indifference. He seemed completely detached.

Ryder pushed back his chair and addressed her. "Can I help you with anything this afternoon, Kathryn? Tina said you wanted to do some stenciling in Frankie's room."

She automatically hesitated. "Oh, I wouldn't want to interrupt your schedule."

"It's too hot at this time of day to work on the shop, and I'm waiting for the baseboards and paint we ordered for the bunkhouse to come in. Don't need to tend the horses 'til evening, so if you need some prep done, I'll be glad to help."

Once, Kathryn would have turned down his help for fear she'd be criticized or somehow disappoint him, but that wasn't true now. She knew exactly what she wanted to do on Frankie's walls, and she knew that she could do a good job of it, just as she knew that she could do a good job with the rest of the house and be of real help to Tina. Why should she turn down help when it was offered?

She looked at Ryder and said, "I'd appreciate that. I've marked off the border on the three walls I want to paint, but the space has to be taped and sanded."

"Consider it done," Ryder said, getting to his feet.

Jake also rose. Looking down at Frankie, he ordered, "Stay out of the way and let Uncle Ryder work. And do whatever KKay tells you."

Frankie nodded meekly, watching, along with everyone else, as Jake strode to the door, yanked it open and disappeared.

Tina sat back in her chair and raised her eyebrows at her husband, who reached for the serving spoon and dipped it into the arroz con pollo. "Mighty good lunch," he said, nodding at Kathryn. Glancing at Tina, he added, "Interesting."

What that meant, Kathryn didn't know, but she felt a little sick, as if the ground had moved unexpectedly beneath her feet. Silently, she rose and began cleaning the kitchen.

* * *

Jake strode out to the barn, his mind whirling with doubts and confusion. He felt like a surly old dog with a bone that he kept burying and digging up. It just wouldn't leave him alone.

Or rather, she. She just wouldn't leave him alone. He'd kept his distance all morning, tracking down Stark and badgering him for advice about Frankie's pony when he should have been working on her car. Through it all, she hadn't left his mind for a moment.

Did she have some man in her life that no one knew about? Or was it possible, as Meredith Burns believed, that Kathryn had never even been on a date? He couldn't accept that at first, but now the idea haunted him, so much so that he feared he'd do something stupid if he spent much more time in her company.

Jake had done some math and figured out that Kathryn had to be in her late twenties. If it was true that she'd never been on a date, someone should do something. Otherwise, he feared that she would spend the rest of her life alone, and what a tragedy that would be.

Someone should definitely do something. But not him.

Resolutely, he turned his thoughts to her old car. A platform of planks laid on the dirt floor of the barn created a firm foundation for his portable lift. He'd moved Kathryn's car onto the lift the very day he'd towed it in. The car now rested about eighteen inches off the ground. The lift would raise the car to a maximum of forty-one inches when he needed to work beneath it, but the current height allowed him to work under the hood without straining his back. He opened his tool chest and started going through the drawers, choosing the tools he'd need and arranging them on a pullout tray. All the while, Jake's thoughts kept circling back to Kathryn.

As he tackled a particularly stubborn bolt, he thought about her father. What kind of man abandoned his handicapped wife and left his quiet, shy, teenaged daughter as her only caregiver? The selfish jerk had to have known how narrow of a life he'd condemned his daughter to, but apparently he hadn't cared.

It wasn't fair. The kind of life she'd led just wasn't fair.

With that thought, he threw his whole weight onto the bolt, which promptly broke off. He knew without even looking that he didn't have a tap bit big enough to move that bolt. Disgusted with himself, he threw the wrench against the wall. What was wrong with him?

Kathryn Stepp's life, including her social life or lack thereof, was none of his business. Still, someone should ask her out. Someone, but *not* him.

He couldn't afford to be dating right now, and even if he could, Kathryn wasn't the right woman for him. She was nothing like Jolene. Besides, it had only been a little over two years since his wife had died. Even if sometimes it felt like forever, another lifetime ago, it was too soon for him to be interested in another woman. He was just missing Jolene. And Houston. And anxious to get his new shop built. He wasn't ready for another serious relationship, and he wasn't sure he ever would be.

Realizing that he could do nothing more until that bolt was drilled out and replaced, he leaned against the fender of Kathryn's old car and wiped his hands with a rag. His throat burning, he dropped the hood of the car and walked out to his truck. Briefly, he considered going into the house, but he didn't want to see Kathryn or anyone else right now. He felt raw and vulnerable. Better to keep his distance until he felt more himself.

He got into the truck and escaped. When he reached the outskirts of Ardmore, he called Tina from his cell phone, in case she needed anything he could pick up on his way to the auto parts store—and because he felt guilty about taking off without a word to anyone. Tina gave him a list so long that she elected to text it to him before she'd even finished talking. He was glad for it. Shopping for her justified his actions somewhat.

After purchasing the correct drill bit for tapping that broken bolt, he started on Tina's list. Nearly everything could be purchased at the home improvement store, but she wanted him to find a particular pair of work gloves for Wyatt at the ranch supply store. After he tried on the gloves and settled on the right size, he picked up a pair for himself and another for Ryder. Then he went to the tack section. Stark had suggested a particular saddle for Frankie, and a certain type of bridle for the pony. Jake could see right away why. The new saddle and bridle would give Frankie greater control of his mount. Jake bought the saddle and bridle, trying not to think about the cost.

Despite his money worries, he was in a better mood by the time he'd arrived back at the ranch house, but then Tina ambushed him the instant he walked through the door with her purchases.

"Listen," she said excitedly, "why don't we let Kathryn drive my old car until you get hers repaired? She wouldn't have to depend on anyone else for transportation that way."

A mobile Kathryn would be a lot easier to avoid. He might never see her again except in passing. Convinced it was a good idea, Jake nodded, but then he heard himself ask, "What about Ryder? That car's *his* transportation. And besides, you still haven't registered the car in Oklahoma. How would you feel if Kathryn got pulled over for having Kansas plates?"

Tina blinked. "I didn't think of that. You're right. I need to take care of getting that vehicle properly registered. Until I do, even Ryder could have a problem."

"Kathryn's shy and skittish, but she's proud, too," Jake went on thoughtfully. "She wouldn't want to let us pay a fine for her. Come to think of it, how do we offer her the car without making it seem like an act of charity?"

"Maybe we could say the car is part of her compensation."

At the rate they were already paying her? He grimaced. "I don't want her to think she's a burden to us."

"No, we don't want that," Tina agreed. "I guess as long as you don't mind driving her around, we ought to just leave things as they are."

"I don't mind," he said quickly, in what he hoped was a casual tone.

Tina suddenly beamed at him. "She's a sweetheart, Jake, a real blessing. You were right about her."

"I'm, uh, glad it's working out," he murmured, feeling oddly exposed all of a sudden. And foolish. What was wrong with him? He knew what he should do. Why couldn't he do it?

Movement at the periphery of his vision caught his

attention. He turned his head to find Kathryn standing near the refrigerator. The look on her face hit him like an arrow to the chest. Shyly pleased, guardedly hopeful, she gazed at him with such warmth that he knew instantly she'd overheard the conversation and put the worst possible connotation on his objections to giving her Tina's old car to drive. The worst possible connotation and the right one. Before he could think of anything to say, she aimed a smile at Tina.

"I've been thinking," she said a little too brightly. "What if we attach the bed skirt to the box springs with Velcro? It won't move around, can be easily removed and will present no problems when you turn the mattress."

"Wyatt will love that idea." Tina turned a gleeful smile on Jake, explaining, "We're going with a simple bed skirt, pleated at the corners. You know, so it's not too frilly." Jake made a humming sound, and she hurried on. "The bed's so big Wyatt worried a bed skirt that completely covered the box springs would make turning the mattress difficult."

"Problem avoided," Jake said, tossing a congratulatory smile around the room while managing to avoid direct eye contact with Kathryn, who muttered something about getting back to work and slipped away.

He quickly handed over Tina's goods then escaped to the barn again, where he began drilling out the broken bolt. Every time he thought of the look on Kathryn's face when he saw her standing there by the refrigerator, he dredged up memories of Jolene and forced his mind back to the job at hand.

He had the broken bolt out and a hoist and chain

rigged to take the weight of the engine when Ryder showed up.

"Dinner's on."

"Already?"

"It's past six."

Jake pulled out his phone and glanced at it. He never wore a wristwatch anymore. He'd broken too many crystal watch faces and demolished too many watchbands. His eyebrows shot up when he saw the time.

"Wow. Okay. I'll straighten up here and be in."

"Can I help?" Ryder asked.

"Nah. Won't take a minute."

"Kathryn's made fajitas. Beef and shrimp." He rubbed his flat belly with the palm of one hand before wandering over to lean against the tool chest, his arms crossed over its smooth top. "Thanks for the work gloves. They're good ones."

"You're welcome."

"Apparently, Rex told Wyatt about them, and he mentioned them to Tina."

"She sure takes care of him, doesn't she?"

He assumed that Ryder nodded, but he didn't look until Ryder suddenly said, "I'm a little envious." Jake shot a surprised glance at his brother. Ryder smiled sheepishly. "When you and Jolene married, I thought it was the dumbest thing you'd ever done."

"What?"

"Well, I didn't understand how marriage could be back then," Ryder admitted.

Jake sometimes forgot that Ryder was five years younger than him, just as Jake was five years younger than Wyatt. He chuckled. He'd married at twenty-three. Ryder hadn't turned eighteen until a few weeks after the wedding. Strange, it felt a lot longer ago than seven years.

"Jolene adored you," Jake said, smiling. "Thought you were the cutest thing she'd ever seen. And it embarrassed you to no end."

Ryder grinned. "She liked to embarrass me."

"She did, but just because she was so fond of you. I thought for sure she was going to pair you up with that cousin of hers."

Ryder rolled his eyes. "No way!"

"She was a pretty little thing."

"With blue hair. And what was with all that eye makeup?"

Grinning, Jake said, "Sometimes I think you're the most conservative Smith of all."

Ryder shrugged. "I just always wonder, what would Mama think?"

Sobering, Jake nodded. He was never sure how much Ryder remembered about their mother. He'd only been five when they'd lost her.

"Mom would be proud of you," Jake told him.

"I hope so." Ryder's gaze slid away, and Jake feared he was thinking about the death of his former sparring partner Bryan Averett. Though it had been nothing more than a freak accident, Jake suspected Ryder still blamed and condemned himself for what had happened.

"Mom would like Tina," Ryder announced. "And Kathryn, too."

Jake's gaze zipped over to his brother again. Ryder gave him a lopsided smile.

"You found a good one there, bro."

Shocked, Jake struggled not to react more than he should. "I think she'll be a big help around here."

Ryder gave him a knowing look. "Uh-huh."

With that, he turned and strolled away. Jake gaped at his little brother as he exited the barn. Had Ryder just let him know that he'd recognized Jake's interest in Kathryn and approved? But Ryder didn't understand.

Kathryn wasn't anything like Jolene. Besides, he wasn't ready. Maybe if he were stable financially, not solely dependent on the ranch and Wyatt's efforts, he could think about…he didn't know what he was thinking or doing anymore, let alone what God was doing.

Jake passed a hand over his face. Part of him wanted to run back to Houston. Part of him wanted to watch Kathryn's eyes soften again and her lips curl into a shy, hopeful smile.

It's only been two years, he reminded himself. She was nothing like Jolene, and he didn't have the money or the time for romance.

Resolved yet again, Jake put away his tools, walked to the house and took his place at the table next to Kathryn.

Chapter Seven

Tina rebuffed Kathryn's efforts to clean up the kitchen. "You've been here long enough today. Go home. Relax. We'll see you on Monday."

Frankie didn't share Tina's sentiment. "KKay, do my bath."

Wyatt scooped up Frankie and tossed the boy over his shoulder, sending Frankie into shrieks of delight. "Doesn't old Uncle Wyatt get a turn to splash water in your face? Besides, we need to clean up your nose. Maybe then you can smell your stinky self."

Frankie clapped both hands over his nose, laughing and protesting at the same time. "Don' clean by nodes!"

Wyatt carted the boy off to the bathroom, shouting at Tyler to join them. Kathryn laughed and waved. Frankie waved back with his free hand.

Overhearing Jake's comments earlier had made Kathryn rethink her behavior. Did she act as proud and skittish around Jake and his family as he'd implied? She very much feared that she did, but no one and nothing in her experience had prepared her for the casual openness and generosity with which this family treated her.

Even before her mother's accident, Kathryn had been shy and careful around others, unwilling to join in group activities. She'd always felt that taking care of things herself was often easier than depending on others. Easier and safer. Kathryn had an abhorrent fear of appearing foolish and incapable. The more she kept to herself, the less reason she had to fear making a misstep. Like Jake, her mother had seen that as pride.

In the past, her fear and pride had driven her to refuse help even when she'd needed it. These Smiths had taught her a thing or two about that. She couldn't imagine a more informed or capable person than Tina, but even she needed help, and Kathryn knew she could be that help. So did Jake. He'd known it before she had.

Kathryn retrieved her bag and looked to Jake. "Ready when you are."

He stuck his left hand in the front pocket of his jeans and pulled out his keys. Kathryn called a farewell to Tina and walked through the door ahead of him, feeling his hand settle into the small of her back as they moved down the outside steps. Her stupid heart flip-flopped inside her chest, but she did her best to ignore it. He meant nothing with his small touches and polite smiles. In fact, sometimes she thought he barely tolerated her. He'd been quick to spare her feelings, though.

"My mother used to tell me I was too proud," she blurted as Jake reached around her to open the passenger door of his truck.

He looked as shocked by her comment as she was. "Hey. Listen. I—I didn't mean anything negative by what I said to Tina earlier. I was just concerned that we not, uh, offend you."

Kathryn smiled wryly at that. "Embarrass me, you mean."

"No. That's not—"

"You got it right," she interrupted gently, bolstering her courage. "I couldn't in good conscience accept the use of a vehicle from your family, not after all you've already done for me. I mean, unless it would benefit you. A-all of you. I mean, you're the one who drives me everywhere. Y-you and Tina."

He pulled the door open, concentrating on the handle as if it required a complicated maneuver to make that happen. "Ten minutes here or there. No big deal." As she climbed up into the passenger seat of the truck, he added, "Besides, it's only right that we help you out when you're doing so much to help us. Tina and Frankie, I mean. Well, me, too, when you think about it, I guess."

Kathryn shook her head. "It's not the same. You're paying me. It's my job to help you. Besides, I could walk back and forth to the ranch. It's not that far."

He settled a stern look on her, his face turning to stone. "I won't hear of you walking, not in this heat. And not when the drive takes so little time."

She nodded, telling herself not to feel so pleased as he closed the door and moved around the truck. He was a good, kind, Christian man. His care and generosity meant nothing except that he tried to follow the precepts of Christ Jesus. It felt *personal*, though, which meant that she was likely having personal feelings about him. Oh, who was she kidding? She'd be mooning over Jacoby Smith day and night if she didn't watch herself.

She'd daydreamed about boys in the past, wondered how it would be if they'd liked her as much as she'd liked them, but she'd always backed away when they'd gotten too close. She was sure that if they'd truly come to know her, they'd have found her as boring as dishwater. That, sadly, hadn't changed.

"So," he said in a conversational tone, sliding behind the steering wheel, "got any plans for the weekend?"

Kathryn nearly laughed. When had she ever had plans for the weekend? She went nowhere and did nothing. She couldn't even call herself a wallflower because she'd have to go somewhere social before she could wind up hiding in a corner. She wasn't pathetic enough to say that, however, so she settled for a negative shake of her head.

His expression blank, he concentrated on backing around the truck and moving it out onto the highway. After several minutes of silence, he abruptly said, "Thought maybe you'd have a date or something."

"Uh, no. Fact is, I've never been on a date."

He looked… She couldn't decide if he was stunned or angry. The next moment, his brows drew together and his lips flattened as if he were in pain, but then he blew out a breath and nodded crisply.

"Oh. Well. You must not see too many movies then."

"Nothing you can't find on TV. I haven't been to a movie theater in years."

"Uh-huh," he said. "You should go with me, then. Us. Me and Frankie, I mean."

Frankie. Ah. She would be overseeing Frankie at the theater, making sure his father could enjoy the movie. Or something. Refusing to acknowledge her disappointment, she pondered the situation. Would Frankie be content to sit still and quiet through a whole movie? She doubted it. Even when he was sitting quietly he was moving, swinging his legs or twisting his body in time to some tune only he could hear, and he naturally spoke in a near shout. Tina had told her that children whose linguistic skills hadn't yet fully developed often did that in a misguided effort to make themselves understood. Shouting, after all, usually drew a quick response. Kathryn figured she'd probably wind up walking him around the theater lobby while his dad enjoyed the movie. Still, even babysitting at the movie theater would be a welcome change from her usual weekend routine.

Her mind began whirling. She needed to look as presentable as possible. Jake, after all, was her boss. One of them, anyway. She didn't want to embarrass him or herself.

"What do people wear to movies these days?"

He shrugged. "Uh, I don't know. Pretty much anything and everything, I guess. Jeans, dresses…date clothes, I suppose. That is, anything you'd wear, like, on a date."

And there was the problem. At this point in time, she had work clothes and little else. She'd had no need for anything more. Still, given enough time, she could devise something. With her sewing machine at the ranch, however, she'd have to start the alterations by hand and finish them during work breaks.

Gathering her courage, she meekly asked, "Would it be possible to put it off a week or so?"

"Oh, sure," he said quickly, nonchalantly. "I just meant we should go sometime. Taking Frankie to the movies by myself is an exercise in futility. But it can wait."

"So, next weekend then?"

He waved a hand. "Next weekend's fine."

"Fine," she echoed, already going through her wardrobe in her mind. Or rather, her mother's wardrobe.

Kathryn had grown taller and filled out since she'd left school, so she could no longer wear the clothes of her youth, not that they'd have been appropriate now. Her mother had owned a lot of nice things, though, and they were close enough in size that she could alter them, even update them a bit. Often, she didn't bother to make the alterations. Who cared how she looked when she was cleaning or cooking anyway? This time, she cared. This time it was more about style than utility.

Date clothes.

"Should I pick you up for church on Sunday?" Jake asked casually.

She startled at the thought. Church clothes. She didn't have any of those, either—nothing appropriate for a Sunday service, anyway. Maybe date clothes could do double duty as church clothes.

"Um, not this week. I—I'll be better prepared next week."

He accepted that easily, nodding. "Right." He lifted a hand, spreading his fingers as if to say he was all out of questions, and they finished the trip in silence.

"See you Monday morning then," he said, bringing the truck to a stop.

Kathryn reached for the door handle. She slid down to the ground and grabbed her bag off the floorboard before backing up a few steps, but then she just stood there awkwardly before blurting, "Have a good weekend!"

"You, too!" he called heartily.

She shut the truck door and hurried up onto the porch. Okay, so it wasn't an actual date, but it was still the first opportunity she'd had in years—decades—to dress like it mattered. Somehow, it did matter, very much. She wasn't even sure she wanted to know *why* it mattered. If she dwelled on that too long, she'd lose her nerve and find an excuse to just stay home.

Her mind filled with possible plans and designs, she didn't even hear the truck back out and drive away or remember unlocking her door and going inside. Suddenly she found herself standing in front of a closet, her gaze roaming over the garments crammed in there. It shouldn't be anything too dressy or ornate, but of course it should be flattering. Very flattering. And contemporary. She didn't want to look like she didn't belong.

She began pulling hangers off the rod and assessing each garment before either tossing it into a pile on the bed or returning it to the closet. A week. She had a week to knock Jake's eyes out. Pausing, she corrected herself.

She had a week to make herself presentable.

Then Jake was taking her to a movie.

She simply could not wipe the stupid grin off her face.

"KKay!"

Kathryn quickly swept the dress she was working on into a rumpled heap of fabric when Frankie and Jake appeared in the laundry room. For two days, she'd been quietly working on the garment during her breaks and free moments. Hopefully they would think it nothing more than another pillow sham or slipcover. She felt guilty for working on the dress at the ranch, but she couldn't ask Jake to tote her heavy old machine back and forth every day. Besides, she made sure to do everything Tina asked of her first. She'd tried to decide if she should cut the long sleeves out of the dress entirely or shorten them, but she remained uncertain. She thought about asking Jake his opinion, but it seemed too much of a personal decision. Maybe she could ask Tina.

"Come out, KKay," Frankie pleaded, drawing her attention back to the present.

"He wants you to come out to the corral to watch him ride his pony," Jake explained apologetically. "I tried to tell him you're too busy, but we're breaking in a new saddle, and he's been working very hard."

Kathryn tried to hide the spurt of alarm that came with thinking of Frankie on horseback, but Jake saw right through her.

"And, yes, we've taken all safety precautions."

"Oh." Pushing back the wheeled desk chair, Kathryn leaned forward, bringing her face down to Frankie's level. "What's your pony's name?"

"Good Boy!" Frankie declared at the top of his lungs.

Perplexed, Kathryn drew back.

"You don't have to shout," Jake admonished. "Remember what we said about using your inside voice?"

Frankie leaned toward Kathryn and in a voice barely above a whisper repeated, "Good Boy."

Still puzzled, Kathryn looked to Jake, whose lips wiggled suspiciously. "Good boy is something Tyler often says to his dog, Tipper. It's an affectionate kind of thing, so Frankie has adopted it as his pony's name."

Disciplining her own smile, Kathryn quickly bit her lips before calmly saying, "Good Boy is an excellent name for a pony. Or a dog."

Frankie turned to his father, clearly making an effort to moderate his volume, and asked plaintively, "S'when doggy?"

Jake rolled his eyes. "When it's weaned. Dr. Burns will let us know as soon as the puppies can leave their mother. They have to stay with her until they can eat solid food and get all their shots. Remember?" Shaking his head at Kathryn, he added, "I never should have taken him to see that litter."

Clearly dissatisfied with that answer, Frankie folded his arms. It was a gesture of Tyler's that Kathryn often saw. Apparently, Jake recognized it, too. Reaching down, Jake brushed Frankie's arms back to his sides.

"Pouting won't make the puppies grow any faster."

Clearly chastened, Frankie bowed his head.

Kathryn shared a glance with Jake then reached out and turned Frankie by his shoulders, saying brightly, "Puppies are such fun. What are you going to name your pup?"

"Doggy," Frankie said, as if that ought to be obvious.

"We'll work on that," Jake commented dryly.

Kathryn bit her lips again to keep from laughing.

"Your pony's waiting," Jake reminded Frankie.

Kathryn quickly stood and offered her hand to the boy, who immediately grasped her fingers and tugged her toward the hallway.

They walked out to the hot, dusty corral. Someone had disked up the dirt to cushion the hard surface, which the heat was busily baking hard again. The little round white pony with brown patches huffed and shifted its weight as Jake led Frankie into the pen. Kathryn stayed outside to lean against the metal-pipe fence.

Jake tightened the girth on the saddle and buckled a helmet onto Frankie's head, but instead of lifting Frankie into the seat, he had the boy grab the saddle horn and hop high enough to get the toe of his left shoe into the stirrup. He then assisted as Frankie threw his right leg over the pony's back and settled in. The boy had some trouble finding the right stirrup, so Jake walked around, always keeping a hand on the little horse, and placed Frankie's foot in the stirrup. Next, Jake simply reached out and untied the reins from a lower rail of the fence and handed them to Frankie.

Her heart pounding, Kathryn noticed that the reins were knotted and Frankie grasped the leather strips on each side of the knot. He laid one side of the reins against the pony's neck and clucked his tongue. When that didn't produce the desired result, he slid his hand down and pulled on the opposite side of the reins. The pony reluctantly turned and plodded along the fence line.

"Good job," Jake called out.

Frankie tried to push the animal to a faster pace. Eventually, the pony picked up its feet. By the second time around the fence, the pony was trotting. Frankie bounced along in the saddle but looked firmly in control. Kathryn relaxed somewhat.

Jake rested his elbows on the top rail of the fence right next to Kathryn, watching Frankie ride. "Stark Burns was sure right about the new rig. Frankie couldn't use his knees properly with the old saddle."

"Frankie seems to know what he's doing now."

"He's getting there."

After a few more rounds, Jake moved into the arena and called out instructions to Frankie, who responded with clear efforts. "Good job, son," Jake called after a few more minutes. "Bring him in now."

Frankie obediently turned the pony and walked it to a halt next to his father. "Get your horse, Daddy?"

"I don't have time to ride out with you today, son. I'll be working late tonight as it is. Maybe tomorrow, though, if you promise not to take off on your own again."

"I pwomise!" Frankie pledged loud enough to make the pony sidestep. Quickly tugging on the reins, Frankie stilled the little horse and turned a beaming smile on Kathryn. "I ridin' good."

"You are," she agreed, "and your pony is very well behaved, too."

Frankie leaned forward and patted the pony's neck. "Good boy, Good Boy."

Kathryn laughed. Grinning at her, Jake told the boy to ride around the corral once more before they rubbed down the horse.

As Frankie turned his mount, Kathryn said to Jake, "I've been meaning to ask you what movie we'll be seeing next weekend."

Glancing at Frankie, Jake folded his arms atop the corral fence and leaned close. "Uh, I haven't said anything to Frankie yet. Kid has no sense of time. You saw how he is about the puppies. If he knows what we're planning, he'll get up every day thinking it's *the* day, and then I'll just have to disappoint him over and over until the time finally comes."

"Right. Should've thought of that."

"Anyway, Frankie seems to generate his own mental movies, no matter what's showing."

That sounded a little alarming to Kathryn. "What do you mean?"

Jake turned and waved over Frankie. He trotted his pony back to the fence and brought it to a stop.

"Son, tell KKay what your favorite movie is."

Frankie put his head back and exclaimed, *"Big Puppy 'n Princess Fly Horses to Moon!"*

Kathryn blinked. "I don't think I've ever heard of that movie."

"No one has," Jake said softly, chuckling. "The big puppy, princess and flying horses are characters from some of his favorite cartoons. He's developed elaborate stories around animated TV characters, and if you make the mistake of letting him tell you about them, you'll be listening *forever.*"

Chuckling, Kathryn nodded. "Got it."

"Big puppy hold wings," Frankie began. "She climb on. Woosh! Up, up, to—"

"There's a reason we don't let Frankie choose our movies," Jake interrupted, sending a droll grin to Kathryn. Turning toward Frankie, he reached for the knot in the reins. "Your pony's hot and tired. He needs a rest. You, too. Besides, KKay should get out of this hot sun." As he spoke, he pulled the reins down over the pony's head and began to lead it, with Frankie still in the saddle, toward the barn. "Tell Kathryn thanks for coming out to watch."

"Thanks you, KKay!" Frankie yelled before smacking a kiss into the palm of his hand and throwing it toward her with a broad, exuberant sweep of his arm.

"You're welcome," Kathryn called, blowing her own kiss to him as she moved toward the house.

Only as she sat down at the sewing machine again did she realize that Jake hadn't answered her question about what movie they would be seeing on Saturday evening. What difference did it make, though? As long as she was with Jake—and Frankie, of course—she'd have a good time. Even if she wound up walking Frankie around the lobby while Jake watched the movie undisturbed, she wouldn't mind. She'd have almost as much fun people watching as movie watching. And she'd look good doing it, too.

Even as she mentally prepared herself for the least enjoyable experience, though, a vision planted itself in her head, a vision of sitting next to Jake in the dark, Frankie snuggled into her lap, Jake's arm spanning her shoulders as the movie played out on the screen in front of them. She wouldn't have the nerve to lay her head on Jake's shoulder, but maybe they would share popcorn and smiles from time to time.

Maybe he'd even hold her hand.

She shook her head.

And Jake thought Frankie's mental movies were far-fetched!

Chapter Eight

Jake repositioned his hat and straightened a crooked belt loop on the waistband of his dark jeans before lifting his gaze to the wreath hanging on Kathryn's front door. He still couldn't believe he was doing this. He'd surprised himself as much as her by suggesting this outing, but when she'd confirmed Meredith's suspicions that she'd never been on a date, he'd wanted to smack every man who'd ever known her. What was wrong with the men around here?

At the same time, Jake knew he shouldn't be the one to ask her out, to let her know she was worthy of a date, which was why he'd brought Frankie into it. Somehow he'd thought he could have his cake and eat it, too, but how did you date a woman, make her happy and still leave her with the understanding that absolutely nothing could come of it? In a few months, maybe, if everything went his way and the garage was turning a profit, he could think about dating, but this was the worst possible time in his life for romance.

Still, he couldn't bear the idea of her sitting home alone weekend after weekend. If only he'd thought it through before he'd opened his big mouth, he might have come up with another way to resolve her situation, but he couldn't seem to control his impulses where she was concerned. Yesterday, in front of the whole family, Tina had presented Kathryn with her first paycheck and mentioned that Kathryn had agreed to attend church with the family tomorrow. Jake had told himself that he would cancel their date when he drove Kathryn home and slipped her his check— he still hadn't told the rest of the family about her raise in pay—but instead he'd arranged the time to pick her up tonight!

To make matters worse, his family had to know it was happening. When he'd asked Tina to tend Frankie tonight, she'd agreed without even asking why or where Jake was going. No one had commented or so much as cracked a smile when he'd come downstairs in his best jeans and long-sleeved, button-up shirt. He'd left the collar open and rolled up his cuffs in an attempt to present a casual image, but everyone had to have known he was going out for the evening and who was going with him.

Squaring his shoulders, Jake lifted his hand and rapped his knuckles against the door. It swung open immediately, as if Kathryn had been standing on the other side waiting for him to knock. The thought made him smile. Then he got a good look at her, and his smile died in astonishment.

She wore a simple navy blue closely-fitted dress with a slightly scooped neckline, short sleeves and a hem that frothed around her slender calves. He thought he recognized that fabric from somewhere, but he couldn't think where. He could barely think at all. She'd pulled the sides of her hair up and back, emphasizing her delicate ears and long, graceful neck. She didn't seem to be wearing makeup, except for some gloss on her lips, but the overall look was sleek and polished, as if she could walk into a boardroom or fancy luncheon with panache and confidence.

Or as if she was ready to go out on a date.

"Wow. I—I mean, you look fantastic."

"Why, thank you." Blushing, she smiled and picked up a small handbag from the arm of the sofa. Moving forward, she caught the doorknob with one hand, pulling it closed as she passed through the opening. Jake stood there like a dumb lump while she took out her keys, locked up and dropped the keys back into her purse. His hand found the small of her back again as they walked across the porch and down the steps side by side. He walked her around to the front passenger door of the truck and assisted her as she climbed up into the seat. Suddenly eager to start their evening, he ran around to the driver's side with long, loping steps and hopped in.

She glanced into the back seat and asked, "Where's Frankie?"

Jake lifted a hand to the back of his neck then got busy starting the truck and backing it out. "Uh, Frankie seemed happier staying home with Tyler, and I thought…" Bringing the truck to a stop, he briefly spread his hands. "You have no idea how long it's been since I saw anything but a kid movie."

She looked at him with a completely blank expression, but then she laughed, prompting his own laughter. Relieved, he drove on.

"I can't even remember what movie I saw last," he admitted.

"I can," Kathryn said.

She named the last movie she'd seen in a theater. He tried to place the title, and it finally clicked.

"That was…" Ten years ago. At least. But he didn't say that because he didn't want to risk sounding as shocked as he felt, so he simply went with "a good one."

She smiled. "It was. I can't wait to see how everything's changed. And I think Frankie's well looked after by his aunt and uncles."

"You don't mind the two of us going on our own?" Jake asked.

She shook her head, eyes shining, and that was enough for him. He'd been right to do this. Nothing meaningful could come of it, of course, but at least she could say she'd been on a date. Besides, he really couldn't remember the last time he'd seen a first-run movie, let alone one made for adults. He couldn't think of anything else to say, so he said the obvious.

"You're right about Frankie being in good hands. Wyatt, Tina and Ryder treat Frankie like he's their own."

"Well, he's a great kid."

"Yeah, I know." For some reason, Jake felt compelled to confide in her. "It bothers me, though, that Frankie sometimes doesn't seem to draw much distinction between his dad and his uncles."

"Oh, but he does," Kathryn insisted. "Do you know what he told me when I tucked him in for his nap after lunch the other day?"

Jake shook his head.

"He told me that his dad is a hero. And his mom, too. He is so proud of that. He called his uncle Wyatt a cowboy and said Ryder was strong." She bent her arms at the elbows, her fists in the air, showing him the gesture that Frankie had made. "Then he said, 'My dad's a soldier. He's a hero.' That boy couldn't be more proud of you."

Pleased, Jake chuckled. "I doubt he worded it exactly like that. We're still working on his sentence structure."

"He got close enough. I certainly had no problem understanding him."

Warmth spread through Jake. He supposed all dads worried about their relationships with their kids to a certain extent, but maybe he didn't have to worry about Frankie preferring his uncles to his father. In fact, he was putting that one little concern aside. Permanently.

"Thanks," Jake told Kathryn. Impulsively, he reached across to squeeze her hand. Smiling, she squeezed back, and that small gesture sent excitement rocketing through him, followed swiftly by doubt and alarm.

Oh, Lord, he thought, *what am I doing? And why haven't You stopped me?*

The last thing he wanted to do was get her hopes up and then disappoint her.

Just this one night. Then he'd level with her. He wasn't looking for a wife. He'd been down that road already. Besides, he couldn't afford even a courtship right now. He might not ever be able to, not so long as he stayed here. Those were just the facts of his life, whether he liked them or not.

Kathryn could not believe the size of the theater. Jake couldn't believe how limited their choices were. Only when they stood in front of the box office window did either of them realize that the one upcoming showing of the film they'd both most enjoy was sold out. Jake sheepishly admitted that he hadn't figured on the whole county turning up for a Saturday night movie.

The only other suitable film would not begin for another half hour, so Jake bought their tickets, and they went inside to sit on a bench while they waited. At first, Katherine used the time by looking around, then a poster featuring a soldier coolly striding out of an explosion caught her eye, and she found herself asking Jake how he'd liked being in the military. Soon they were in deep conversation. Talk naturally progressed to his late wife.

"Jolene was something," he said, smiling. "All woman and all soldier. In some ways, she seemed indestructible. I mean, I thought about getting killed while I was away on deployment. You have to. And I even thought about her getting killed, but not really. You know? It just didn't seem possible. Or maybe I just didn't want to think about it."

"I can understand that," Kathryn told him, thinking how different Jolene must have been from her. Irrationally, she hoped that Jake wasn't thinking the same thing.

"Is her death why you and your brothers moved to Loco Man rather than let someone run the ranch for you?"

He shook his head. "It was another tragedy that prompted our move, but that's a long story." He pulled out his phone then and checked the time. His eyes went so wide that Kathryn instinctively looked up at the clock on the wall of the theater lobby. The movie had started nearly thirty-five minutes ago!

Jake jumped to his feet and threw up his hands.

"What do you want to do? Go in late? Try another movie?"

She didn't know what to do. "How bad do you want to see a movie?"

He just looked at her, then he started to laugh. "I don't, really. Other than our original choice, I'm not sure there's anything showing that wouldn't embarrass us with bad language and other junk. These days you can't tell unless it's G-rated, though."

"I'm definitely a G-rated kind of girl," she said, not at all disappointed. It wasn't about the film for her, anyway. It was about... Finally, she faced the facts squarely. It was about spending time with Jake, getting to know Jake, and it always had been.

He reached down to take her by the elbow and help her to her feet. "Let's just go, then. We can, I don't know, grab a couple of milkshakes maybe?"

She could've danced out on air because he hadn't said he'd just take her home, but she made herself nod serenely. "Sounds good."

He drove her to a chain restaurant famous for milkshakes. They sat in a booth, sipping the deliciously indulgent drinks, laughing about their lousy timing and discussing the general state of modern movies.

After a while she said, "You never did explain what brought you and your brothers to our little corner of the world."

He told her about Ryder then, about the freak accident that had killed Ryder's sparring partner. Kathryn was shocked and saddened by the story, but not disturbed. Ryder, in fact, disturbed her the least of all the Smith brothers. He was big and strong, yes, but less grizzly bear than teddy bear, all cute and no bite.

Wyatt, on the other hand, as the eldest brother, was definitely the boss at Loco Man Ranch. He'd have intimidated Kathryn terribly if she hadn't witnessed firsthand how caring and indulgent he was with his wife.

"Ryder must've been horrified by what happened," she mused. "He's a gentle giant. I can barely see him as a martial arts enthusiast, let alone a fighter."

"I know. Right?" Jake shook his head, as if still puzzled over how it had happened. "It's not at all like him, but he let himself get talked into competing by a promoter. He didn't want to hurt anyone and was determined to be a skills fighter. He believed that if he honed his skills enough, he'd win on the basis of technique alone. And it worked until that kid, Bryan— he was just barely twenty-one—broke his neck while they were practicing a new move. I can't tell you how deeply it affected Ryder. The press wouldn't leave it alone, even after an investigation proved Ryder had done nothing wrong."

"So you brought him to Oklahoma to get away from all that," Kathryn surmised.

Jake swirled the inch or two left of his milkshake, nodding. "Moving was Wyatt's idea, but it felt like God was pointing us this way when we found out Uncle Dodd had left us the ranch. I considered staying behind in Houston, but for what? Who? We don't have much family left, just some distant cousins and each other. And Frankie loves, needs, his uncles."

"I'm not surprised about Wyatt. As for Frankie, his uncles and you must be all the family he remembers. Of course, now he has Tina and Tyler, as well."

"True. But I'm not sure what you mean about Wyatt."

Kathryn thought about it before carefully answering. "Wyatt's the decisive, authoritative, take-charge type. I'm not surprised he drove the decision to move here. I imagine he can be, well, forceful when it comes to getting his way about something."

Jake chuckled. "He's more reasonable than you seem to think. Granted, he's the big brother to his bones, and he's used to running a business. Several, actually. He took over for our dad, in more ways than one, well before Dad passed on. And it's true that he didn't want me and Frankie to stay behind, but he wouldn't have pressured me on it. Too much."

She laughed at that, repeating his words for emphasis. "Too much."

Jake grinned. Then his gaze shifted to meet hers evenly, and he folded his arms against the tabletop, dropping his voice a notch. "So if Ryder's the gentle giant, and Wyatt's the authority figure, what does that make me?"

The last words she'd said fell out of her mouth again of their own volition. "Too much." Knowing that sounded ridiculous, she dropped her gaze and softly added, "Too much of everything. Handsome, kind, generous, hardworking. Masculine."

For a long moment, she could neither lift her gaze nor breathe. Her heart seemed to have stopped beating. She couldn't believe she'd found the courage to say all that. Then he reached across the table, picked up her hand and pressed it between both of his. Suddenly, she could function again. Looking up, Kathryn found him smiling tenderly.

The waitress chose that moment to drop off their

check. Jake sat back, picked up that little slip of paper, glanced at it and looked to Kathryn.

"Guess it's time to go."

Disappointed and at the same time absurdly happy, she nodded, made sure she had her handbag and slid to the edge of her seat as Jake moved to his feet. This time, when Jake reached down, she gave him her hand, thrilled beyond words when he kept it until they reached his truck.

Too much.

Jake continually pondered her words as he drove them back to War Bonnet.

Too handsome. Too kind. Too generous. Too hardworking. Too masculine, whatever that meant.

He didn't think it was bad, any of it. He thought that perhaps he had misread her early on. She didn't dislike him. She liked him *too much.*

For a woman like her, that must be unsettling, and it made this little outing a very bad idea. That being the case, he shouldn't smile about it, but he couldn't help himself, so he tried to focus on just how badly he had fouled up the evening.

"I'm really sorry about the movie."

She sent him a gentle smile. "Don't worry about it. The milkshake was compensation enough. I shudder to think how long it's been since I last had a simple milkshake. Besides, you were under no obligation to take me to a movie after Frankie dropped out."

Increasingly uncomfortable with that fiction, Jake shifted in his seat and came clean with her. "About that. I never really intended to bring Frankie. I just said that because I didn't want you to think this was…"

"A date?" she finished for him.

He shot her a surprised glance. "Yeah, I guess. Sounds stupid, I know. But, look, I'm not in a position to get serious about anybody. It's only been a couple years since Jolene. A-and the truth is, the shop is eating my lunch. I've got to get it up and operational before..."

"Before?"

"I don't want you to take this the wrong way, but I have to get the business established before I run out of money."

"And working on my old car is putting a crimp in things."

"No, no, I'm not losing anything but time working on your car, and Ryder is helping me with the construction on the shop to make up for that. But what it if doesn't work out? I think there's enough business in the area to pay the bills, especially if I don't have to borrow to finish the building, but it's not a given. I could wind up supporting the shop instead of the other way around. Frankly, I shouldn't even be spending money on movies, let alone kids' saddles and special bridles, not until I know the shop is going to be at least self-supporting. I—I just shouldn't be dating right now."

"So if you didn't want me to think this was a date, why didn't you bring Frankie?" she asked.

Grimacing, Jake said, "He's a disaster in a movie theater. He talks to the screen at the top of his lungs, and half the time he's on his feet. I just said I was including him because..." He tried to think of the least embarrassing way to say this. "I didn't think you'd go if it was just the two of us."

"And why would you think that?" she drawled wryly. "Just because I locked myself in the car when you stopped to help me? Or was it how long it took me to look you in the eye?"

Jake realized with a shock that she was teasing, but that she was also well aware of how her behavior must have come across. He had to smile. At both of them.

"Let's just say it's been a long time since I asked a woman to go to a movie with me. Or anywhere else."

She laughed softly and admitted, "I probably wouldn't have."

Jake shot a glance at her and caught her self-deprecating grimace.

"Go to a movie with you, I mean. Or anywhere else. Your fiction about including Frankie allowed me to make peace with my desire to go by telling myself that it was work related. I think I always knew you hadn't originally intended to include him, but I did expect you to bring him along after you added him to the equation."

Surprised again, but also pleased, Jake asked, "Then why did you come with me after I showed up without him?"

Again, she gave him that wry smile and tone. "Because sitting at home alone isn't nearly as much fun as I pretend it is."

A bark of laughter burst out of him. She laughed, too. Within moments, they'd settled into a comfortable silence.

Then abruptly she said, "I take it this is your first date since your wife died."

He blinked at that, his smile fading. "You know, you're right. I've met a few women, called them up on the phone, chatted with them, even flirted a little. I just didn't…" He looked at her, realizing what the problem had been. "I just wasn't ready. I'm not real sure I am now either. Or that I ever will be."

"So I guess it was a first for both of us," she said softly, ducking her chin. "And the last."

The sound of disappointment in her voice cut Jake to the quick. He wished he'd made a real date of it, an actual invitation, dinner and a movie, maybe even flowers. At the very least, he should have put some serious thought into the event, especially if it was to be the only one. And it ought to be. He had no right to usurp any woman's time and emotions until he knew they had a chance for something more.

The silence grew increasingly thick, not strained exactly but rife with...awareness. Thankfully, they reached her house before the atmosphere became unbearable.

"I'll get your door," he announced, bailing out on his side. It was the gentlemanly thing to do, after all. She waited while he rushed around to open the door for her. He backed up, giving her room to get out. As he followed her up onto the porch, properly seeing her right to her door, he kept that distance, his nerves jittering beneath his skin.

Without a word, she took her keys out and unlocked the door. Then she turned to him, smiled and said, "Can I ask you something else?"

"Sure."

"If, as you say, you're not in a position to be dating, why did you take me out?"

He did not know how to answer that. If he gave her the same excuses he'd been giving himself, it would sound like pity, and he couldn't let her think that. For one thing, it wasn't true. Maybe she hadn't dated, but

Kathryn had made a life for herself all on her own. She had a kind of strength he'd never before encountered, and he was only just realizing it.

He stood there, staring at her, his tongue glued to the roof of his mouth, and wrestled with what he knew to be true. He'd asked her out because he'd wanted to be the first man ever to do so and because she needed to know that she was lovely, completely worthy.

When she mumbled a farewell and started to turn away, he couldn't let her. She deserved more than that, better than that. His hand at her waist, he turned her back to him. She looked up with those big, deep green eyes, and he knew what had to happen next.

Shifting closer, he brought his other hand to the center of her back, between her shoulder blades, but he didn't pull her against him as he wanted to do. Instead, he simply bent his head and kissed her. She closed the small distance between them, leaning forward until she met his chest, her arms at her sides. Thrilled, he tightened his embrace incrementally until she lifted her arms and slid them about his neck.

It was the sweetest kiss ever, as tender and pure as his very first. He'd been about thirteen and so nervous he'd shaken like a leaf in a gale. That girl's face had long ago faded from his memory, but he did recall that there had been about a foot between them and they'd both blushed furiously afterward. Still, that first kiss had been one of his sweetest, most sentimental memories. It paled in comparison to this.

Everything will pale in comparison after this.

That thought jolted him, breaking the kiss and shoving him back several inches. Kathryn looked as stunned as he felt, her eyes wide, fingertips hovering tremulously over her lips. Before he could even blink, she bolted, disappearing into her house. He stood for several moments staring at the wreath on her door before he realized that the evening was at an end and he should go. Still, more seconds ticked away before he could make himself draw breath, turn and walk back to his truck.

Frowning, he told himself that he'd just done the most stupid thing he'd ever managed in his entire life, but he couldn't seem to stop the pleasure that filled him. All the way home, he vividly relived every instant of that kiss. She'd bolted afterward, yes. As shy, skittish and careful as Kathryn was, he had expected no less, but before that, she'd kissed him back. She had kissed him as much as he had kissed her.

And his head was still spinning because of it.

Chapter Nine

Looking at her reflection in the mirror the next morning, Kathryn wished once again that she had not agreed to attend church with the Smith family.

The kiss had kept her awake all night. As a girl, she'd dreamed and dreamed of her first kiss, but she'd never come close to imagining the sensations or emotions that Jake's kiss had evoked in her. She'd felt cherished and beautiful, as if she'd been made for that exact moment, that one man. To him it had undoubtedly been nothing more than a good-night gesture. To her, it was nothing less than a wonder.

Now, in the light of day, she didn't know how she was going to face him. He'd been frank about the fact that they had no future, but that didn't keep her from wishing it could be otherwise. Would he be able to read her foolish sentiment in her eyes? After all, he was a mature, experienced man. He'd been married, for pity's sake. A spinster's first kiss couldn't mean to him what it meant to her. Even if he didn't see how she felt, Tina surely would.

She and Tina had quickly become good friends.

Kathryn was glad for that, but she worried Tina would take one look at her now and *know*. Not that she had anything to be ashamed of. A woman her age could reasonably be expected to have been kissed.

But no woman could be expected to have had a first kiss like *that*.

Oh, how she wished she hadn't agreed to attend church with the Smiths this morning.

She thought briefly of feigning illness, but she didn't want to lie, so she was ready and waiting at the appointed time. To her relief—and disappointment—it wasn't Jake at her door. Instead, Tina, smiling and lovely in a summery print dress, looked approvingly at Kathryn's, the same one she'd worn last night with Jake. She hadn't had time to refashion anything else, but she was already planning her next project, if only to have something different to wear to church in the future.

When she got to the SUV, Kathryn found that the boys occupied the third-row seat. With Tina and Wyatt in the front, that left the second row for Kathryn alone. Frankie greeted her enthusiastically.

"KKay pretty!"

She smiled at him. "Thank you." She hoped his father would be of the same opinion, instead of wondering why she'd chosen this particular dress again. Then she silently scolded herself for even thinking about Jake. He'd made it clear that he wasn't interested in romance at this point in his life. She couldn't let herself think of anything more than friendship with Jake. And she dared not allow thoughts of *the kiss* to enter her mind.

That proved even more difficult than expected when

they arrived at the church. Jake and Ryder stood out-side, waiting for them. Wyatt stopped the SUV right in front of them. Ryder opened Tina's door while Jake did the same for Kathryn. He smiled impersonally as she exited the vehicle, then he ducked inside to free Frankie from his safety seat and pull him out of the au-tomobile. Tyler managed for himself, and Jake moved back to allow Ryder to shepherd the boy toward the church. Tina followed, while Wyatt parked the vehicle.

Kathryn couldn't keep her gaze off Jake. He looked impossibly handsome in his dark jeans, white shirt and tan suit jacket, a brown tie knotted at his throat. He wore a cowboy hat as if born to wear it, and every time she looked at him, she remembered *the kiss*.

With those memories came awkwardness, but she didn't know what to do about it. Running away was not an option this time. Thankfully, no sooner did Jake set Frankie's feet on the ground than Frankie grabbed her hand, drawing her attention away from his father.

"KKay come to me," he said, tugging her toward the church.

Jake strode after them, speaking to Frankie. "Come *with* me. Kathryn doesn't need to see your classroom, though."

"I don't mind," Kathryn countered quickly.

Without another word, Jake followed her and Frankie into the church foyer, Ryder and Tyler holding the door for them. Frankie tugged Kathryn down a hallway flanking the sanctuary. Behind her, she heard Jake say, "I'll take Tyler. Y'all save us seats."

They reached Tyler's classroom first. He went in with a quick parting wave. Frankie's room was tucked into a corner near the nursery suite, and he insisted on showing Kathryn every corner of the colorful space. She made the appropriate noises of approval and appreciation, until Jake impatiently swept her out of there and back the way they'd come, his hat in his hand. Music was playing by the time they slipped into the end of the pew next to Wyatt and Tina. That didn't stop Wyatt from leaning forward, looking past Kathryn and speaking to Jake.

"So where did you get off to last night? You ran out before I could ask this morning."

Tina jabbed Wyatt with her elbow. At the same time, Jake shushed him, a finger lifted to his lips. In that moment, Kathryn realized that the family knew nothing of the evening she'd spent with Jake. Tina might—probably did—suspect, but she couldn't know for sure. Kathryn had told Tina that the dress she was working on was for Sunday, and it was. However, it was also for the movie, which Kathryn hadn't mentioned for fear Tina would assume a context that didn't exist.

Beside her, Jake fixed his attention on the front of the sanctuary and kept it there, which allowed her to focus somewhat on the service. To her surprise, the music, message and familiar rituals calmed and comforted her. She knew that Jake would not be asking her out again, and her disappointment was keen, but she couldn't be angry or resentful with the one man who had taken her out on a date.

Jake Smith had unknowingly brought change to her life, change for the better. She had a job she enjoyed, good friends and more financial security than she'd known in a long while. Plus, her car would soon be running again.

And she'd been on a date, or as close to one as she was likely to get.

She would be forever grateful.

After the service, Tina hurried off to collect the boys while everyone else stood around the crowded foyer and chatted. The Billings family joined them, patriarch Wes with his bride, Alice, on his arm, along with Rex and his wife, Callie, and Meri and her husband, the veterinarian Stark Burns. Kathryn knew Alice best of all. The only time Mia had ever left their house after her accident was by ambulance or to visit the office of Dr. Alice Shorter, now Billings. Those visits had proved so arduous that Kathryn had been discouraged from attempting any other outings, but upon occasion, Kathryn herself had used the services of Dr. Alice.

"It's so good to see you, Kathryn," the doctor said warmly, "and in such good company."

Kathryn smiled and nodded, desperately trying not to be aware of Jake at her side. It was enough that she didn't feel out of place, out of her depth. The sense of belonging, of being part of group, was a novel sensation for her, but she knew very well that she wasn't part of a *couple*. Even if Jake hadn't leveled with her, his cool, casual demeanor would have told her that their one date would not be repeated. Even as they left the building and Jake's brothers teased him about his "mysterious disappearance" the night before, Jake remained calm and impassive.

"You know, what I do is none of your business," he replied easily to their prods.

Kathryn was glad for his circumspection. Had his behavior or tone implied any intimacy between them, she would have been hard-pressed to maintain her composure.

Finally, Wyatt announced that everyone should "load up." The whole family trooped out into the parking lot. While Jake crawled into the back of Tina's SUV to buckle Frankie and Tyler into their safety seats, Kathryn waited outside, Tina next to her, chatting about the service. Just as Jake stepped down onto the ground and straightened, Tina placed a hand on Kathryn's arm and asked easily, "Joining us for Sunday dinner?"

Jake stiffened, prompting Kathryn to refuse. "Oh, no, thank you. I have a lot to do."

Flashing her another impersonal smile, Jake moved off toward Ryder. "See you in the morning then."

Both relieved and disheartened, Kathryn got into the SUV and buckled up. She told herself that she'd gotten through her first meeting with Jake and his family after *the kiss* and her secret was safe. No one ever needed to know that she'd developed a killer crush on Jake, not that anything could come of it. He'd made that very plain.

After carefully thinking over all he'd said and done, she had concluded that she'd been a safe first date for him after his wife's death, a way to test his readiness to begin again. No doubt he had asked her out precisely because she could have no expectations where he was concerned. He'd been up-front about it. Besides, a man like Jake could spend time with any woman he wanted. He certainly didn't need a plain gal like her. It was enough that her first kiss had been the stuff of legends. Even if it proved to be her only kiss, she would treasure the memory always.

* * *

After Sunday and the way that kiss had affected him, along with his tendency to act on impulse with her, Jake decided that keeping his distance would be best for both of them. It spared him temptation and her the idea that he was ready for more in a relationship than he was. He still didn't understand what drew him to her, given how different she was from Jolene, but it didn't matter. He was in no position to pursue any woman now, and if the garage wasn't a success, he might never be.

As the oven that was August cooled into the slightly more tolerable temperatures of September, school started. Jake asked Ryder to take over driving Kathryn back and forth to the ranch, telling everyone who would listen that he was too busy to drive her himself. Kathryn hadn't turned a hair. She privately accepted a check from him every Friday with downcast eyes and a silent nod of thanks. During meals, she remained quiet and subdued, saving her smiles and conversation for Tina and Frankie, who missed Tyler dreadfully during the day. Jake told himself that Kathryn was fine.

They were both fine, even if he felt hollow inside.

As September moved along without any rain, Jake's composure felt as dry and fissured as the landscape, and his brutal work schedule—mornings and evenings on the shop, afternoons on Kathryn's car—wasn't helping. Kathryn's car was slow going, mostly because he was determined to spare her every penny he could, and that meant searching out the cheapest parts and sometimes opting for used ones, which often required reconditioning.

By the second Monday of the month, he felt ready to shatter. After a couple hours of cleaning an old part, he was ready to install it, but then he realized he'd mislaid his work gloves. Those gloves gave him a sure grip and helped prevent busted knuckles. He'd taken his extras to the shop site so he didn't have to manage those concrete blocks with bare hands. He went to his truck to see if he'd left his new gloves, or even an old pair, in there. All he found was a pair of heavy, mangled cotton gloves. Making a mental note to buy a few extra pairs of leather ones to stash around the place, he paused to think where his good leather gloves might have gotten to. Suddenly, he had a clear memory of leaving them atop his dresser.

Despite the need to avoid Kathryn, Jake quietly entered the house and climbed the stairs. Neither Kathryn nor Tina was anywhere in sight. He went first to Frankie's room. His son napped peacefully beneath the ceiling fan in his bedroom. Jake tiptoed to his own room and found the gloves exactly where he remembered leaving them the night before. Congratulating himself on accomplishing his task without inadvertently walking into the lion's den of Kathryn Stepp's gentle presence, Jake slipped downstairs and headed for the back door, only to freeze when he heard Tina's voice coming from the master bedroom.

"So he did kiss you."

"All right, he kissed me," Kathryn confirmed softly.

Jake had no doubt about which *he* the two women were speaking. He told himself not to listen, that eavesdropping was wrong and dangerous, that nothing good could come of overhearing their conversation. Like so many other times, he ignored his own best advice where Kathryn Stepp was concerned.

"I knew it!" Tina crowed. "And?"

"And what? It meant nothing."

"Oh, please," Tina scoffed. "I know these Smith brothers. Everything means something to them."

"Not in this case."

"What was it like?" Tina asked.

For several seconds, Kathryn said nothing, then she spoke again. "Unique."

Jake frowned. *Unique?* His kiss was unique? What did that mean? He folded his arms and leaned his head forward slightly in the hope of hearing better.

"That's it?" Tina prodded.

"I don't know what to tell you. I have nothing to compare it with."

Jake pressed back against the wall, imagining Tina's shock.

"You're telling me that you can't compare Jake's kiss to any other because you've never had any other?" Tina demanded.

"Jake was my first date. If you can even call it a date."

"What do you mean?" Tina sounded indignant, almost angry. "A date is a date."

Jake waited for Kathryn to reveal that he had tricked her into going out with him. Instead, she said, "We meant to go to a movie, but we wound up just having milkshakes."

"Milkshakes!" Tina squawked. "What is this, 1950? Were you wearing bobby socks and a poodle skirt?"

Jake squeezed his eyes closed in a grimace. Tina was right. He hadn't even given the woman a proper first date. Hearing Kathryn's laughter didn't ease his mortification one bit.

"No, I was wearing a very nice dress. You saw it. The blue one."

"He took you for milkshakes in *that*?" Tina demanded. "What is wrong with him?"

Jake rather wanted to know that himself.

"It didn't mean anything," Kathryn said again, her voice breathy and hushed. "I think I was a safe choice for his first date since the death of his wife. That's all."

A safe choice? It was all Jake could do not to snort in derision.

"What a dope!" Tina exclaimed.

Kathryn ignored that, asking, "Where did Wyatt take you on your first date?" Jake got the feeling the answer was important to her.

Tina stammered for a moment. "It—it was…well, w-we…come to think of it, we didn't actually date at all, not in the strictest sense of the word."

"But you've both dated others, right? So you both knew exactly what you were looking for."

"I dated quite a bit when I was younger, and of course, I was married before," Tina told her. "And Wyatt, well, just look at him. I'm sure he dated lots of women before he met me, but no one ever knows exactly what or who they're looking for, not that either of us was particularly looking for anyone. I, in fact, was definitely not looking."

"But you must have known what you didn't want, at least," Kathryn pressed.

"Absolutely. I didn't want anyone like my ex. I guess, now that I think about it, I wanted someone like my stepdad."

"Dodd Smith."

"That's right."

Kathryn seemed to consider that before slowly saying, "I don't want anyone like my father. Beyond that…"

"Have you even known anyone else to compare your father to?" Tina asked.

"Beside the Smith brothers? Not really. Well, a little. Teachers and people like that."

"But you haven't been in school in years," Tina pointed out.

"It has been a long time," Kathryn agreed, "and I was awfully shy back then. I didn't know anyone well."

"Back then?" Tina chuckled. "And now?"

"Now I know you," Kathryn pointed out, and Jake could hear the smile in her voice.

"And I know you," Tina responded warmly. From the sound of it, they were hugging.

Jake hurried away before they discovered him. Tina was correct that Kathryn deserved much better than Jake had given her, but he didn't dare try to offer her anything more. If he took her out again, let alone kissed her again, she'd expect more than he could give her. It wouldn't be fair, to either of them.

Sick at heart, Jake went back to the barn, but he couldn't concentrate on the work. He recalled how she'd looked this past Sunday in a simple gray knit dress with hardly any sleeves. The knit had hugged her curves lovingly, its gently bowed neckline resting just below her pretty collarbone. He hadn't been able to take his eyes off her. Memories of his "unique" kiss had kept him awake that night. It wasn't the first time.

Suddenly, he felt as if he were drowning. The lingering heat, the frustratingly slow process of building the shop while working on Kathryn's old car, the uncertainty of his financial future and this nameless ache inside of him poured out in a flood of frustration. He had to get away, if only for an hour or two.

Resolved, Jake returned to the house, glanced casually at Kathryn and Tina, who were preparing the evening meal, and reached for his hat.

"Sorry, ladies, I won't be home for dinner. Tell Frankie I'll see him soon as I get back."

"If you're going into Ardmore—" Tina began sharply, parking her hands at her waist.

"Not this time," Jake interrupted apologetically. "There's a guy with a bunch of junked cars in a gully on his place. I'm going to see what I can find there. I'll make a run to Ardmore for you later, though."

"Don't bother." Tina looked at Kathryn. "Want to take a drive into Ardmore tomorrow?"

Kathryn bowed her head, her lips clamped firmly between her teeth, but then she nodded. Tina waved a hand at Jake, dismissing him. Clearly he had sunk in his sister-in-law's esteem. He couldn't blame her. He wasn't thinking too highly of himself just then.

Jamming his hat onto his head, he went out the door. A couple hours later, he had removed several small parts from the rusting jumble on a property east of town. It was almost dinnertime, and he needed to get something into his stomach. He drove into War Bonnet and walked into the diner, where he took a seat on a stool at the counter.

A vaguely familiar-looking man soon claimed the stool next to him. He smiled at Jake and said, "You're just the fellow I've been wanting to see."

Jake didn't place the guy until he removed his hat and laid it, crown down, next to his elbow. "It's Goodell, isn't it? With the Cattlemen's Association."

"That's right. Clark Goodell. And you're one of the Smith brothers."

"Jake."

The two shook hands. The waitress dropped off glasses of water, slung menus at them and said she'd be back. Jake opened the small bill of fare, but Goodell didn't reach for his menu, his gaze fixed on Jake.

"I hear that KKay Stepp is working for your outfit now."

Shocked, Jake frowned at the other man. "Yeah, so?"

"I'm just wondering…is she seeing anybody?"

Ice water suddenly poured through Jake's veins. "And what concern is that of yours?"

"Look," Goodell said with a slight smile, "Kathryn is highly thought of around here."

"Not surprised by that," Jake growled.

"She was completely devoted to her mother," Goodell went on, "but I'm told that she was seen recently at the movie theater in the company of a man."

"And that would be your business how?"

Clark Goodell looked away. "We went to school together."

"Okay. And?"

Goodell fixed him with an implacable gaze. "And I want to know if you or one of your brothers has a claim on her."

It took every ounce of Jake's willpower to keep his fists tucked beneath the counter. "My oldest brother is married."

"So that leaves him out," Goodell prodded. "What about you and the other one?"

Jake took a long drink of water. Looked like the joke was on him. The men around here weren't blind and stupid, after all. For Kathryn's sake, he was glad of it, but knowing that her options were about to explode crushed him in a way he hadn't expected.

"She's not seeing anyone," Jake made himself say before draining his water glass. With that, he got up and walked out of there.

His appetite had vanished, and he was starting to feel sick to his stomach.

He had the feeling that would get worse before it got better.

Chapter Ten

Exhaustion pulled at Kathryn as she dropped down onto the sofa in her living room the next evening. After their trek to Ardmore that morning, Frankie had run rampant all afternoon. Kathryn had done her best to distract and entertain him, but Tina had finally reached the end of her tether and sent him to his room. He hadn't even taken a nap. He'd just lain in his bed babbling some fiction about horses, dogs and talking cars. Dinner had been a tense affair, with Tyler whining about homework, Frankie pouting, Wyatt distracted with the beginning of construction of the carport and Jake silent and brooding throughout.

Kathryn was starting to think Jake resented her presence. In fact, she'd begun to wonder if she could continue as an employee at Loco Man Ranch. In answer to a pointed question from Wyatt, Jake had estimated that her car would be ready within another week or so. Kathryn had told herself that it might be best if she went back to the home care agency as soon as her car was drivable. Then she'd come home just now to find a letter from her father in her mailbox.

He warned her that he had consulted an attorney. Though declaring that he didn't want to force her hand, he revealed that he'd had the house evaluated by a Realtor. All he was asking was that she put the house on the market—as if that wouldn't destroy her world. Her plan to offer him monthly payments to buy out his interest in the house would be completely unworkable if she went back to the home care agency. What was she going to do? Work two jobs, perhaps? If she could find two jobs around here.

She needed to work up some numbers, but before she could do that, a knock sounded on her door. Her heart in her throat, she jumped to her feet.

Had her father come in person to demand that she accede to his wishes? His mail had come postmarked from Tahlequah, but that was only a little over four hours away. With the second knock, Kathryn lurched toward the sound.

Seeing a cowboy hat through the high, narrow window in the door, she threw the bolt and yanked the door open, only to find herself staring at a stranger. Of average height, with a blocky build and dressed in the standard cowboy fare of boots, jeans, button-up shirt and hat, he smiled at her, displaying dimples. He swept off the hat, revealing short, sandy hair atop a squarish face with twinkling blue eyes.

"Hello, Kathryn."

Something clawed at the back of her mind, a memory long abandoned. With it came a name—and complete shock. Only the dimples and the blue eyes remained of the classmate she'd once known.

"Clark Goodell!"

The dimples deepened. "The same. How you doing? It's good to see you. You look great, by the way."

Her hand went instinctively to her hair, the top part of which she had pulled back in a short, thick ponytail. She had decided to grow it out again and was trying her hand at various styles in the meantime. "I do? I—I mean, I just got home from work, so…"

He leaned a forearm against the doorframe. "Loco Man Ranch, right?"

"Yes."

"How's that going?"

She shrugged. "I cook and clean, help with the kids, do some decorating. I like it."

"Glad to know it. I also hear you're getting out and about."

"Oh. Uh. Yeah, I guess."

"I know you've been seeing someone," he said softly.

"What?"

"Weren't you at the movie theater in Ardmore with someone a while ago?"

Kathryn's jaw dropped. "Oh. That." She didn't know how to explain her outing with Jake, so she retreated into silence.

"I was just wondering if it's exclusive," Clark said smoothly. "Jake Smith didn't seem to think so, but he looked kind of stumped when I brought it up."

Kathryn's heart thumped. "You spoke to Jake about me?"

Clark had the grace to appear abashed. "I figured if you were seeing someone it was probably one of the Smith brothers."

Her chest ached so deeply that she could barely

breathe. "No," she whispered. "I'm not seeing anyone exclusively."

"I'd like to ask you out for dinner, then," Clark said, smiling.

Kathryn blinked, beyond speechless.

"You were always so sweet and shy," he went on. "I can see that hasn't changed. So, dinner? Would Friday work for you?"

For some reason, she wanted to cry, but that would be foolish. Clark had only confirmed that Jake wouldn't be asking her out again. She had tried not to let Jake's rejection hurt, but it did. She knew herself well enough to know that if she retreated now, she'd spend the rest of her life grieving what could never have been. Lifting her chin, she pasted on a smile.

"Friday will be fine."

Clark hung around for several more minutes, setting the time and place for their dinner together. He gave her a card with his phone number on it. Kathryn saw that he worked for the local cattlemen's association. He was probably a friend of Jake's. Her disappointment escalated. How many ways did Jake have to tell her that he lacked interest in her? She supposed it would be the same with Clark. He'd discover how dull and unexciting she was, and that would be that. Still, she couldn't find the strength to take back her acceptance of his invitation. She had never learned how to be that rude.

Over the next two days, she hastily made over another outfit and resigned herself to an uncomfortable evening in the company of Clark Goodell. Clark had always been a polite, well behaved boy in school, with a strong desire to attend Oklahoma State University. She hadn't even realized he'd returned to War Bonnet after college, but then she hadn't thought about it one way or another. And now she was going to dinner with him. Belatedly, she realized she should've made the date for Saturday rather than Friday. Had she done so, she wouldn't have had to explain to Tina why she needed to leave early, and Tina wouldn't have announced the same at lunch on Friday.

"Kathryn has to get ready for a dinner date, so we'll be eating frozen pizza tonight."

The boys cheered. Tina fixed them with a stern look, adding, "And salad that Kathryn will prepare before she leaves."

Frankie sighed. Tyler said "Yum," but the curl of his nose revealed his true feelings.

Kathryn couldn't help smiling. These boys were a constant source of joy to her. She would miss them. The thought brought her up short, but she knew then that she would leave Loco Man and everyone on it. For her own peace of mind, she must. From now on, she would concentrate on saving her home, as she'd done before she'd met Jake Smith.

"Kathryn will need to leave earlier than usual," Tina said.

Everyone instantly looked to Jake. Ryder was texturing the walls in the bunkhouse, as the smears of white on his clothing attested, and Wyatt had scheduled a teleconference with a tax consultant. Tina would be busy with the kids and the evening meal. Jake, after all, was the logical choice to drive Kathryn home. He was working on her car. It was only right that work for her be delayed for her convenience. Yet Jake said nothing until he finished his meal and rose to leave the table.

"Back to work," he muttered, striding for the door, as if he hadn't heard a word Tina had said.

Kathryn's face flushed, the breath catching in her lungs.

Ryder gave her a sweet smile. "I'll be happy to knock off early enough to get you home in time for your date."

"Thank you," she managed, but she couldn't look anyone there in the face. Rising from the table, her appetite gone, she began cleaning the kitchen.

Behind her, Tina said, "I have a better idea. Kathryn, why don't you drive my old car? I got it registered and tagged recently."

Kathryn paused. "But that's Ryder's transportation, isn't it?"

"Oh, I don't mind," he told her. "There's plenty of transportation around here."

"It's settled then," Tina decreed. "You'll drive the sedan until your car's ready."

Tears burned the backs of Kathryn's eyes. Yes, she must leave this job as soon possible. She told herself that she would miss Tina most of all, but she knew that wasn't so. It was Jake—just the loss of the dream of Jake—that would inflict the deepest cut.

She managed to get through the rest of the day and drive home in Tina's little sedan. It had been weeks since she'd last driven a vehicle, and Tina's car was a definite step up from her small, bare-bones coupe. She told herself how pleased she was to have some measure of independence returned to her, but she was no good at lying to herself. As she dressed and prepared for the coming evening, she tried not to think of anyone or anything except what she was doing at that very moment.

Clark arrived right on time, and she found herself in yet another pickup truck. He drove her to Healdton for catfish—excellent catfish, as it turned out. Clark was an entertaining conversationalist and a gentleman. He put her at ease early on, and that didn't change even when he confessed that he'd had a crush on her in high school and was sorry when she'd dropped out.

It was a surprisingly pleasant evening, and after he drove her home, he kissed her good-night standing on the porch of her house, just as Jake had done. Except it wasn't the same at all. Clark promised to call her and left her smiling, despite the depression that had settled over her. She'd expected to be relieved at the end of the evening. Instead, she wanted to cry. She finally had a social life, and Clark was a very nice man. Still, she hoped he wouldn't ask her out again, at least not for a while.

To Kathryn's surprise and puzzlement, she had two more invitations that weekend, both by telephone and both of which she turned down. It was easier to refuse when the invitation came by phone. One of the men was younger than she was and complained about the dearth of women his age around War Bonnet. The other was several years older and the divorced father of three. She was flattered at the sudden interest, but dating now seemed like a lot of bother for no good reason. Maybe later, when she was over Jake, she'd feel differently.

She'd never been able to talk to anyone else the way she could talk to Jake. Even with Tina, she felt foolish and inadequate at least part of the time. With Jake, she hadn't just been at ease, she'd been herself. Her true self. Obviously, her true self hadn't been engaging enough to hold his interest. She should just accept that. She would accept that.

Clark was waiting for her when she arrived at church on Sunday. She'd considered not going, but when she'd refused Tina's offer to pick her up, Tina had laughed and hugged her.

"What am I thinking? You can drive yourself. We'll meet you there."

Kathryn hadn't known how to tell Tina that she didn't want to be anywhere Jake might be, but with him ignoring her like she didn't exist, it didn't make much difference, anyway. When she saw Clark, she almost turned around and left again, but then he smiled and hurried toward her.

"Thought we might sit together."

At least she wouldn't have to sit next to Jake while he looked at everything and everyone but her. Kathryn smiled at Clark. "I'd like that."

They took a seat several rows ahead of the Smiths and on the other side of the aisle. After the service, Clark offered to drive her home.

"Oh, I drove myself," she said apologetically.

Just then, Frankie ran up and threw his arms around her. "KKay! We fishin' today!" Frankie reported. "You come."

"It sounds like fun," Kathryn began.

Before she could say more, Clark kissed her on the cheek and said, "I'll call you."

She nodded, and he went on his way. Focusing entirely on Frankie, she refused to so much as glance in Jake's direction. "I'm afraid I can't go fishing with you today. I have things to do at home."

Frankie dropped his head, but then he snagged Kathryn's hand and towed her toward the door in Tina and Wyatt's wake. She was aware of Jake trailing along behind them, but neither acknowledged the other. When they reached Tina's SUV, Frankie urged her to get in.

"Sweetie, I'm not riding with you today. I drove myself here, and I'll have to drive myself home."

"Come on, son," Jake said, sweeping around Kathryn to pick up the boy. "I'll belt you into your seat."

"No!" Frankie bawled, shoving at Jake's hands. "KKay do it!" Jake made an exasperated sound and plopped the boy into his safety seat. "KKay do it!"

Jake backed out of the vehicle and walked away without another word. Kathryn had helped Tina buckle in the boys the previous week, so she had little difficulty getting the restraint system in place. Again, Tina invited her to Sunday dinner, but again Kathryn declined. It had become something of a ritual.

"I'm sure you've had enough of me for one week."

"Are you sure it's not the other way around?" Tina asked softly, frowning.

Kathryn couldn't let Tina think that. "Not at all. You're like family to me now."

"And even family needs some personal time," Tina remarked, smiling.

Kathryn nodded, but home had never felt quite so empty as it did that hot Sunday afternoon in mid-September.

Jake didn't like to work on Sundays, but he couldn't seem to relax that afternoon. Watching Kathryn with Clark Goodell had told him that her date with the local cowboy had gone well. They seemed at ease together, and Kathryn had never looked finer. Jake suspected that Tina either knew the details of the situation or soon would, but he didn't dare ask. He told himself that it didn't matter, that it was all for good, but something more than curiosity gnawed at him. He tried to think of Jolene, to call up the old grief and feelings of loyalty. That didn't help. Memories of Jolene left him with a sense of gratitude and melancholy but did nothing to blot out the vision of Kathryn sitting beside Clark in church.

Desperate for distraction, Jake went over every detail of his business plan. He looked at his estimates and adjusted the numbers to reflect the additional outlay of Kathryn's salary. That reminded him that he still hadn't informed the rest of the family of her raise in pay. Today he wondered why he bothered to keep it a secret.

At first, he'd feared that the extra pay would betray his interest in Kathryn, but now that she was dating Clark Goodell, that was no longer an issue. No one could say that Goodell let moss grow under his feet. He must have beat a path straight from the diner to Kathryn's door. And she obviously hadn't turned him away.

Suddenly, Jake wanted to throttle someone, but the only villain in this piece was him. He'd tricked her into going out with him, then told her in no uncertain terms that he wouldn't be dating her or anyone else again any time soon. And then he'd kissed her. He'd tried to convince himself that they could be friends without expectations of more in the future, but that friend stuff would only work if he could maintain a safe distance, and after that kiss he wasn't at all sure he could. God knew he'd tried, but the best he could do was to skulk around her wishing it could be different and feeling like a ghost.

He tried to imagine some way to make it work, but what if the garage failed? If the garage failed, he and Frankie would wind up back in Houston, or they'd have to move to some other big city where he was sure to find work. How could he ask that of Kathryn, knowing how difficult she found it to meet strangers and make friends?

Good grief, he was thinking of marriage. The very idea shocked him, but what other option did he have with a woman like Kathryn? She deserved marriage and would remain alone for the rest of her life before she'd settle for anything less. He didn't want her to live her life alone, so he had to accept that she'd wind up with another man, probably sooner rather than later. She was entitled to every happiness, and he wanted that for her. Still, he couldn't seem to keep a civil tongue in his head when he saw Kathryn on Monday.

She served up a massive submarine sandwich for lunch. He took one bite and complained, "Did we run out of mustard? This is as bland as cardboard."

Kathryn silently set the mustard jar in front of him. He proceeded to drown his portion of the sandwich in the tart yellow stuff, then he had to choke it down with everyone glaring at him. Later, when Ryder asked to borrow Jake's truck, Jake started digging out the keys and grumbling.

"Man, I'll be glad when that stupid car is finally running so we can get back to something like normal." He tossed the keys onto the table.

Stiffly, Kathryn turned from the sink and walked over to the peg where she'd hung her bag that morning, saying, "That's not necessary." She pulled out the keys to Tina's little sedan and carried them to Ryder. "It's your car," she said. "I only need it for twenty minutes a day, and even driving it for that long makes me uneasy."

Ryder glowered at Jake then took the keys from Kathryn. "Thanks, Kathryn. I'll return the keys to you later, or drive you home, whichever you prefer."

Nodding, she smiled wanly and went back to the sink.

Ryder sent Jake another hard look, shaming him to the point that he called her that night and apologized.

"It's all right, Jake," she said in that soft, shy voice that made him want to reach through the phone and wrap his arms around her. "You're under a lot of pressure." Then she changed the subject. "Tina and I have been talking about taking Frankie to the lake to swim. I don't know how much help I'd be, though. I never learned to swim myself."

"You never learned to swim?" Jake yelped. "Well, you must. Everyone needs to know how to swim." He opened his mouth to say he'd teach her, only to remember at the last moment that he was keeping his distance. And Clark Goodell was not. "Maybe Clark will teach you," he heard himself say, then he wanted to bite off his tongue. She said nothing to that, so after a moment of sheer agony, he asked, "How's that going, by the way?"

"I don't know what you mean."

"I saw you sitting with Clark Goodell in church on Sunday."

"Oh. That went just fine."

She wasn't willingly going to give him anything

more. He should have expected that, given how introverted, cautious and closed off she could be.

"How about your dinner date? That go okay, too?" He had to ask.

She was slow to answer. "It was very good. If you like fried catfish."

"I love fried catfish." And yet he hadn't been the one to take her to dinner. "Apparently not as much as old Clark, though."

"How did you know Clark was the one to take me to dinner?"

Stunned that it might have been someone else, Jake stuttered. "I—I j-just assumed. You had a dinner date on Friday and you were sitting with him in church on Sunday. Seems logical the two are connected."

"I know he spoke with you," she said.

Jake closed his eyes. He could've warned off Goodell, could've staked his own claim, but that wouldn't have been fair. To anyone. "Yeah, Goodell spoke to me at the diner."

"The diner? You discussed me at the diner?" Her voice shook. "That's gossip central. And what else did you discuss at the diner, Jake? My father the drunk who can't keep a job? How my mother had to drive to Duncan and back every day for work to support us? That she crashed her car one rainy night and would need constant care from that point on? Maybe how he walked out on us."

"It wasn't like that," Jake said, grimacing at the thought of all she'd been through. Her family must have been the subject of much gossip at one time, and a shy woman like Kathryn would find being the talk of the town mortifying.

"Oh, of course. That's old news," she retorted. "Maybe this time you heard that he's threatening to sue me for *his* half of *my* house!"

Good grief. No wonder she had despaired when her car had broken down. After all he'd done, her father had some nerve trying to get money out of her for her house. She must be worried sick about that.

"No," Jake told her quietly. "I didn't hear any of that. Clark only wanted to know if you were seeing someone. Apparently, whoever saw us at the movie theater recognized you but not me. I knew by the way Clark reacted that he would be calling you, then when I saw you sitting with him in church yesterday…"

"You naturally assumed it was Clark who took me to dinner on Friday night."

Jake forced a light, congratulatory tone to his voice. "Apparently, he knows all the good places to eat around here."

"It was good," she said, adopting his tone. "Maybe I should take you there after you're finished with my car. To thank you."

Part of him rejoiced. Part of him quailed. But what harm could a meal do? They had eaten many meals together. Before he could accept her invitation, she spoke again.

"Oh, no. That's no good. That would just be me doing what you did. I'll give you the address of the restaurant. Then you can go whenever you want. With whoever you want."

Jake closed his eyes, fighting with himself. He considered saying that they could go together once the shop started paying off, but that took for granted that the shop would provide income and that she would wait.

What if she waited and it didn't happen? What would that cost her? A chance at happiness? A chance for marriage and a family of her own? He couldn't do that to her.

Resigned, he put away his justifications.

"I'll have your car ready soon," he told her softly.

A moment later he ended the call, as depressed as he'd ever been in his life.

Chapter Eleven

Looking up from the sewing machine, Kathryn glanced at her phone sitting on the counter at her elbow. She'd set a timer then ignored it, and now Tina had to come in, probably to tell her that she needed to start lunch.

"I'm so sorry. I was just going to finish this one row of stitching then get back to work, but I got caught up in the project and lost track of time."

Tina chuckled, waving away her concern. "No need to apologize. What are you working on? Another gorgeous dress, I see."

Kathryn shook out the silky brown fabric, holding the garment by the narrow sleeves, which she'd shortened to elbow length.

Tina fingered the fabric. "Oh, my. Your mom had excellent taste."

"I always thought so, especially with her work wardrobe."

"What did she do?"

"She was an insurance agent. She started as a secretary and taught herself the business. She knew everything there was to know about all kinds of insurance—auto, home, health, life… I shudder to think what would have happened to us if she hadn't had excellent health insurance."

"She was a well-dressed insurance agent," Tina said.

Kathryn sighed. "I just wish she'd had some more casual things."

Tina's eyes lit up. "We have to go shopping."

Kathryn threw up her hands. "Never fails. What did we forget?"

"Not for the ranch," Tina declared, pulling Kathryn up by the arms. "I need to buy Tyler a few more things for school, and Frankie's jeans are already too short. He'll never make it through the fall with what he's got now."

"Grows like a weed, doesn't he?"

"He does. So we're going shopping. And we're not taking the boys."

"But—"

"Not taking the boys," Tina repeated firmly. "I have their sizes, and it's easier to choose for them when they're not around. And I want you to have all the time and freedom you need to shop for yourself."

"Oh, I don't know if—"

Tina held up a finger. "I'm pulling rank on you, girl-friend. I'm the boss, and I say we're going shopping."

Kathryn could only smile and say, "Yes, ma'am." She couldn't help wondering what Jake would have to say about her leaving Frankie behind, though.

When Tina informed Wyatt at lunch that he would be staying home to oversee the contractor and watch the boys that afternoon, he glanced around the room and meekly said, "Yes, dear." His brothers laughed, but Wyatt just winked and said, "Feisty little thing, isn't she?"

Tina smirked, ignoring him. "Kathryn and I will put chicken and potatoes into the crockpot, so we can get dinner on in a matter of minutes after we get back. If you'll just have the boys ready, we should make prayer meeting without any problems."

"We can do that," Wyatt said, looking at Jake, who merely nodded.

"It's settled then," she decreed, rushing Kathryn toward the door. Once they were outside, Tina laughed and said, "That was easier than expected."

Kathryn made one more protest. "I should be working, not shopping."

"Shopping *is* working," Tina countered dryly.

Kathryn got in the SUV.

Five hours later, exhausted but the proud owner of three new outfits—all purchased at deep discount—Kathryn desperately wanted a shower. Tina, on the other hand, had resisted buying anything for herself. Once or twice she'd seemed tempted by certain items of clothing, but then she'd just sighed and put them back. When Kathryn asked why, Tina made a face.

"I'll get too fat to wear them. You don't know how good you have it being thin. You're the kind who won't even put on weight when you're pregnant."

Kathryn didn't say that her chances of ever having a child were slim to none. She'd be thirty before she knew what hit her, and it wasn't likely that she'd marry any time soon. Jake's face popped up before her mind's eye, his gaze warm above that gorgeous smile. Mentally shoving away the image, she'd scolded Tina for thinking she was overweight.

"You're not fat. You're shapely. I, on the other hand, have the figure of a stick."

"Rub it in, why don't you?" Tina drawled.

Kathryn laughed and helped Tina stow their purchases in the SUV. When Tina straightened and reached up to pull down the tailgate, all the color drained out of her face and she suddenly collapsed against the bumper. Crying out, Kathryn caught her and lifted her up enough to sit on the edge of the SUV's baggage deck.

"Tina! What's wrong?"

Tina put a hand to her head. "Dizzy. Guess it's the heat."

"Let's get you home."

"You'd better drive."

Tina reached into her handbag for her keys and handed them over. Kathryn walked her around to the passenger seat before hurrying to take her place behind the steering wheel. She turned on the air conditioner full blast and stopped at a drive-through for a cool drink, but halfway home Tina gasped and put her hand over her mouth. Kathryn quickly pulled over so Tina could throw up. Afterward, Kathryn gave her a mint, helped her lie back her seat and broke speed limits getting home to the ranch.

Because the construction crew was working on the carport, Kathryn parked the car in front of the corral, which was directly across from the house.

"Where's Wyatt?" she demanded of the workers, but the voice that answered her was Jake's.

"He and the boys drove into town," he said, striding toward her from the barn. "What's wrong?"

"Tina's ill. Help me get her in the house."

"I can manage on my own," Tina said, sliding down

to the ground. She did look better, but Kathryn wasn't taking any chances, and neither was Jake. He rushed to Tina's side and would have carried her into the house if she hadn't threatened him. "I'm fine. Put your hands on me, though, and I'll kick you in the shin."

She wouldn't have hurt him, of course, and he did put his hands on her, but he settled for wrapping an arm around her back and escorting her inside, Kathryn hurrying along beside them. Tina insisted on brushing her teeth. Kathryn followed her, standing outside the bathroom door in case Tina felt faint again. They returned to the kitchen, where Jake waited anxiously. Tina sat at the table.

"How about a cold glass of iced tea?" Kathryn offered, feeling Tina's clammy forehead with the palm of her hand.

Tina made a face. "I think I'd rather have a soft drink. And crackers." Always worried about her weight, Tina seldom drank anything sweetened with sugar, and lately she'd stopped stocking colas and soft drinks with artificial sweeteners.

"Are you sure?"

"I think it might settle my stomach."

Kathryn went for the crackers while Jake retrieved the soft drink.

"I think I should call Wyatt," he said, delivering the cold, canned beverage to her.

Tina shook her head. "No. I'll be better in a minute."

"After you finish that, go lie down," Kathryn urged. "I can manage dinner."

"I'll help her," Jake volunteered.

Kathryn shook her head. "It's mostly ready. I'll just open some canned vegetables and call it done."

"Well, I'm not leaving until Wyatt returns," Jake said, pulling out a chair.

Kathryn went about getting the dinner together, while Tina munched crackers and sipped her clear, sparkling beverage. Wyatt and the boys came in just as Kathryn was pulling plates from the cupboard.

"Tina is ill," Jake announced immediately.

Concern stamped on his face, Wyatt went to her, tossing whatever he'd bought in town on the table. She got to her feet as he approached, smiling.

"I'm fine. Just a little upset stomach. Probably the heat."

He wrapped his arms around her. "You sure, sweetheart?"

"Absolutely."

Wyatt smiled down at her, seeming to relax. "I love you," he said, and the two kissed.

Jake shot to his feet and out the door. Obviously, Kathryn reflected sourly, he couldn't wait to get away from her. At least he'd stayed put until Wyatt came.

"Dinner in ten minutes," Kathryn called after him.

"We got popslickels for 'zert!" Frankie declared to Kathryn.

She pulled her attention away from Jake's retreat and focused on his son. "That's wonderful. Let's put them in the freezer so they don't melt."

"Yeah," Frankie said, adding emphatically, "I want red."

Kathryn chuckled. "I'll remember that." She sent both boys off to wash their hands and went back to preparing dinner.

Tina asked Wyatt to go out to the SUV and bring in the shopping bags, then insisted on setting the table before separating their purchases into two piles. Ryder came in and went to wash up. Kathryn was putting the food on the table when Jake came in again and went to the kitchen sink.

"When we're done here," Tina said to Kathryn, "Wyatt and I will clean up so you can get home. I know you probably want to shower before prayer meeting."

"Are you sure you should go to prayer meeting tonight?" Kathryn asked, concern tugging at her.

Tina chuckled. "I keep telling everyone, I'm fine. I'll feel even better *after* prayer meeting."

Kathryn smiled. "That's always how I feel, too."

"Oh, wait," Tina said. "Why not just get ready here? You can use one of the guest rooms upstairs."

Kathryn glanced at the parcels on the floor. "I can do that, I guess." No one would have to drive her back and forth this way or pass her the keys to Tina's old sedan again.

They finished the meal, Jake again as silent as stone. Kathryn carried her shopping bags upstairs and dropped them on the bed in the room at the end of the hall before going straight to the shower. Just feeling clean again cooled and reinvigorated her. Tina brought up a blow dryer and curling iron, as well as a few other essentials. She seemed almost fully recovered from her earlier bout of sickness.

After drying and curling her hair, Kathryn pulled out a newly purchased sundress, removed the tags and put it on. Thankfully, she'd worn sandals that morning. She loved the way the dress swirled around her legs, falling to midcalf. Tying the string belt at her waist, she tossed the faded denim jacket that came with the dress over her shoulders and went downstairs to join the others. Everyone commented on how pretty she looked in her new dress. Everyone but Jake. He barely glanced at her before heading outside.

She felt frostbitten, his cold indifference a kind of death of all her hopes and dreams. Determined not to cry, she pasted on a smile, stiffened her spine and filed out with everyone. Once again, Jake and Ryder traveled in Jake's truck. Kathryn rode in the SUV with the others. At the church, Kathryn found herself sitting between Tina and Ryder. She told herself she was glad. It made it easier for her to ignore Jake. He certainly had no trouble ignoring her.

Kathryn was surprised that neither Wyatt nor Tina asked for prayer after Tina's bout of illness that afternoon. Ryder also seemed bothered by that, leaning forward at one point and sending his brother a meaningful look. Wyatt's response had been to take Tina's hand in his. Well, Kathryn certainly understood the desire for privacy. Perhaps Tina was not quite as fully recovered as she pretended, however, for as soon as they reached the foyer, Wyatt announced that he was taking Tina and the boys straight home. That left Jake and Ryder to drive Kathryn to her house.

She rode in the back seat, staring at the text message that had come in while her phone was silenced in church. Clark had written to say that he was out of town and hadn't had a moment to call due to constant meetings but didn't want her to think he was ignoring her. Kathryn knew that if not for Jake Smith, she'd be thrilled, but it was difficult to swoon over Clark when the man who had alternately enthralled and wounded her sat within her immediate line of sight.

Arriving at her house a few minutes later, she was

surprised to see an unfamiliar luxury sedan parked in her driveway. Jake pulled up on the passenger side of the other vehicle.

"You've got company," Ryder said needlessly.

"So I see," she murmured, opening her door. "Thanks for the ride." She quickly alighted and walked around to the car, wondering who her visitor might be and fearing the worst. Perhaps it was her father. More likely his attorney. Mitchel Stepp had never owned a luxury anything.

A tall, slender man with very little blond hair and a nervous smile got out on the driver's side to greet her. Wearing a short-sleeved sport shirt, pleated slacks and black dress shoes, he looked distinctly uncomfortable.

"Kathryn?"

"Yes."

He put out his hand. "Jay Wilson. I was just about to leave."

Jay Wilson, the divorced father of three who had called her some days ago. As an introvert herself, she knew one when she saw one. She shook his hand.

"You won't remember me," he said, as if that explained everything. "I was several years ahead of you in school. I called on Saturday."

"Oh, yes." She forced a smile.

"I was wondering," he said, "if you'd reconsider going out with me. There's…there's a recital. My daughter's a piano student. She's only eleven, but she's quite good."

"You must be very proud of her," Kathryn said quickly. She heard a door open and glanced over his shoulder in time to see Jake get out of the truck. Frowning, she switched back to Jay Wilson. "Normally I would be happy to go with you to your daughter's recital, but I'm…" She lowered her voice, quickly adding, "I'm, well, I'm interested in someone else."

Jay Wilson glanced back at Jake. "Ah. I see. Sorry to have bothered you."

"Not at all," she hastened to say, smiling apologetically. "I should have told you when you called. I was just so flattered by your invitation…"

Bobbing his head, he took swift leave of her, flags of color flying across his cheekbones. His car was halfway down the drive before Jake reached her side.

Scowling at the sedan, Jake asked, "Who was that?"

"A nice man," Kathryn answered tersely, starting toward the house.

Jake kept pace with her. "That's not Clark."

"No, it's not. Clark is out of town."

He stopped at the bottom of the porch steps. "That guy asked you out, didn't he?"

Kathryn just smiled and went up the steps. She had no desire to go out with Jay Wilson. He was attractive enough, and she couldn't deny that his persistence flattered her. Moreover, she was thrilled to think that men, some men, found her attractive, but it was unfair of her to go out with anyone, Clark included, until her heart was her own again.

That didn't mean her social life was any business of the one man who'd made it clear she was not for him. She went into the house without another word.

Jake sat silently beside Kathryn at church on the following Sunday and mentally kicked himself for the thousandth time. He'd opened a proverbial Pandora's box by denying his interest in Kathryn. He'd answered the question of just one man, and now suitors were coming out of the woodwork. For days now, he'd tried to be glad for her but could only be miserable for himself. Would every single man within driving distance be on her doorstep now? At this rate, she'd be married by winter.

He tried not to look at her, but she was so stunning, elegant and sophisticated in a formfitting brown dress with a flat bow on one shoulder. He couldn't help himself. Of course, she wasn't sitting beside him so much as she was sitting beside Tina. He'd just managed to get between her and Ryder. Another stupid move on his part. He couldn't concentrate on anything but her, and she wouldn't even be sitting here next to him if Clark Goodell had attended church this morning.

His own jealousy and possessiveness shocked Jake. He had no right to such feelings, and silently confessing them did little to alleviate his gloom, especially when a man whom Jake didn't know approached Kathryn immediately after the service and received a warm welcome. Tall, blond and muscular, he seemed a little young for Kathryn, but the two hugged and stood talking animatedly together. Trying not to glower, Jake fetched Frankie from his classroom, only to find the pair still talking when he returned to the foyer.

Jake had sense enough to recognize his own jealousy and fight it. Surely his preoccupation with Kathryn was not healthy. It bordered on obsession, and that bothered him. He'd never had these issues with Jolene.

He and Jolene had come across each other in the course of their assignments. Rank being no issue, they'd both flirted a bit. They'd been comfortable together from the very beginning, and Jake had never known a moment's concern about Jolene liking him. In fact, she had asked him out the first time, rather than the other way around. Neither of them had dated anyone else from that point on, and their mutual affection had quickly become so obvious, a superior officer had suggested that marriage would be best for their careers. They'd gone shopping for a ring the next day and were married in uniform by the base chaplain just over four months later.

Jake reflected morosely that Kathryn seemed more comfortable with Clark and this new fellow than she was with him. Knowing it was all his fault didn't help a bit. The whole thing made Jake's head and chest ache.

"Grinding your teeth won't make her yours," said a voice at his shoulder. Jake spun on his heel, turning his glare on his big brother. Wyatt lifted both hands. "Just saying."

Jake turned away, scoffing, "You don't know what you're talking about."

"No? Wasn't that long ago that you and Ryder advised me to go after Tina."

The fact of that made Wyatt's words no less galling. Both of his brothers obviously read him much more easily than he'd assumed, but neither of them understood his turmoil.

"It's not the same," Jake hissed. "Kathryn is nothing like Tina or—"

"Jolene?" Wyatt finished for him. "What difference does that make? You're not trying to replace Jolene. The people we love aren't replaceable. You're moving on to a new relationship, something unique. Unless you let yourself get beat out by a college kid."

Ignoring the rest of Wyatt's words, Jake seized on

what felt most pertinent. "College kid?" Jake glanced at the man talking to Kathryn. He was muscular and fit but quite young.

"Rex says his name is Derek Cabbot. Apparently, he plays college football in Texas."

Cabbot. The name flitted through Jake's mind, lodging in a specific memory.

"Is he any kin to a Sandy Cabbot?"

"Rex said he's Sandy Cabbot's grandson, but I have no idea who Sandy Cabbot is."

"He's a former client of Kathryn's."

"Ah. Sandy probably misses her," Wyatt remarked casually. "We would if she left us."

She'd said she might go back to the home care agency once her car was repaired, and it was drivable now, though the brakes felt spongy to him, and the clutch was slipping. Plus, he thought she could have an exhaust leak. That was all beside the point, however.

He shook his head at his brother, his gaze on Kathryn. "I can't get involved with anyone right now."

"I don't see why not."

"My finances are stretched to the limit," Jake admitted, finally looking at his brother. "If the shop doesn't quickly turn a profit, I... I don't know what I'll do."

Grinning, Wyatt clapped him on the shoulder. "Try a little faith."

At the rate he was going, Jake thought glumly, it was going to take a *lot* of faith. Heaps and tons of faith.

More than he could find.

Chapter Twelve

"I'm taking Tina and Tyler home now," Wyatt said. "Ryder and I will see to lunch. Want me to take Frankie with us?"

Jake nodded, preoccupied with Wyatt's advice. Faith. Was it faith to expect that God would give him what he wanted when he wanted so much? He wanted Kathryn, but he wanted the financial stability to support her, too, and he wanted it here, near his brothers. On the other hand, how was he to know if he didn't take at least a few steps in the direction he wanted to go? *I'll understand if You slap me down, Lord,* Jake prayed silently, taking his son by the hand and walking straight toward Kathryn and her friend.

"Guess Frankie will go with you," Wyatt muttered, chuckling.

Jake barely heard him, his troubled mind trying to make sense of what he knew, what he felt and what he wanted. Kathryn might well bring him up short. God knew she had no reason to feel kindly toward him after the way he'd alternately ignored and grumbled at her.

Frankie, as usual, showed no restraint. He threw his

arms around Kathryn as soon as they reached her. She stooped to hug him then rose to split a smile between Frankie and Mr. Athletic.

"Frankie, this is my good friend Derek. Derek, this is Frankie."

Derek went down on his haunches, smiling at Frankie and offering his hand. "Nice to meet you, Frankie."

"S'it nice mee' you!" Frankie practically bawled into Derek's chiseled face, shaking his hand.

Looking up at Kathryn, Derek quipped, "Kind of like talking to Grandpa. He thinks everyone is as deaf as him."

She laughed. Apparently, Frankie didn't like the attention Derek was paying her any more than Jake did. Grimacing, he gripped two fingers on Derek's hand and pumped it again. Derek grinned and pretended to shake blood back into his fingers.

"Wow. That's quite a grip you've got there. How old are you?"

Frankie held up three fingers.

"You're a big boy for three. Maybe you'll play football in a few years. What d'you think?"

Frankie shook his head. "I can't frow."

"No? That's okay. You'll be able to knock over the guy who does throw the ball, and that's the most fun part."

Both Frankie and Kathryn laughed as Derek pushed up to a standing position once more. That was all Jake could take. It was bad enough Derek Cabbot could charm Kathryn; he didn't have to charm Frankie, too. Jake stepped up next to Kathryn. For a fraction of a second, he hesitated, then—like Frankie—he did exactly what he wanted to do. He slid an arm loosely around her shoulders and placed the other hand on top of Frankie's head, effectively claiming both. Kathryn stiffened and shifted slightly away from him but otherwise did not react.

Jake nodded at Cabbot and said to Kathryn, "About ready to go?" He patted Frankie's head, smiling down at him. "We need to get this one fed so he doesn't miss his nap."

Derek Cabbot's eyebrows rose halfway to his hairline. Kathryn bit her lips then made the necessary introductions.

"I hope your grandfather is well," Jake said, after Kathryn had told him what he already knew.

"As well as he can be, I guess," Cabbot replied.

"He always rallies when you're around," Kathryn said to Cabbot. "He enjoys your visits so much. Tell him I'll call soon."

"He'll like that," Derek said to her. "You know how he loves the telephone."

They laughed about Sandy Cabbot's fondness for the telephone. Irritated, Jake put on a smile. Finally, Kathryn said farewell to Derek and moved toward the door, out of Jake's reach. He and Frankie followed close behind.

"When did you meet Derek Cabbot?" Jake wanted to know.

"When he visited his grandfather. He's such a thoughtful grandson," Kathryn said brightly, but her arms were as stiff as rods at her sides. "Sandy lives for that boy."

Boy. Suddenly Jake could breathe a little easier. He reminded himself, however, that Clark Goodell was no boy, and Kathryn clearly preferred Clark to him at the moment.

Tina hailed them as soon as they stepped out the doors, insistently waving them over to join the group around her. Mentally sighing, Jake followed Kathryn to Tina's side. Tina stood with Wyatt, Tyler, Ryder and Ann Billings Pryor's family.

"Ann and Dean are inviting everyone over to their place for dinner next Sunday," Tina announced.

Ann looked at Kathryn and Jake. "It's cooled off some, and the new school year's started. We thought an end-of-season cookout was in order. Is 6:00 p.m. too late for y'all?"

Y'all. As if they were a couple. Him and Kathryn. Jake tried not to take that as some sort of validation. Instead, he simply looked to Kathryn, keeping his expression bland. "Fine by me. What about you?"

Kathryn seemed to struggle for a moment. Being the center of attention would always make her uncomfortable, but he suspected this was less about that and more about him. He couldn't blame her. He'd done a very good job of keeping his distance and discouraging any connection between them. He probably ought to keep on doing that, but he just didn't have the energy or the heart for it anymore. Besides, what difference would one evening in the company of others make?

All the difference he could squeeze out of it, he decided abruptly.

To his relief, she finally nodded and said to Ann, "I look forward to it."

Ann beamed a smile all around the group. "It's a date then. Next Sunday. Six o'clock."

"Let us know what we can bring," Tina said. "Kathryn's a marvelous cook."

As color rose to Kathryn's cheeks, Wyatt said to Tina, "Now will you go home?"

She rolled her eyes and trekked off toward the SUV, followed by Wyatt, Tyler and Ryder. Jake walked Frankie and Kathryn toward his truck.

"Tina's right," he said. "You are an excellent cook."

Kathryn bit her lips and bowed her head but said nothing. She didn't speak again until they reached her house, and then she merely murmured her thanks before getting out of the truck and going inside.

Faith, Jake thought.

Would faith put money in his bank account? Or make up for the damage he'd already done? Or keep Kathryn's father from forcing her to sell her house? He'd been worried about the latter, and the truth was that if he should somehow overcome all the barriers he'd erected and win Kathryn's heart, he'd be adding one more overwhelming financial responsibility to his already overburdened budget. Yet somehow, he just couldn't find the sense to care about that anymore.

Now if only he could undo the damage he'd done.

"It's running," Jake said the next morning, "but you'd better test-drive it before we call it done." He opened his fingers to show the key lying on his palm.

It had been so long since Kathryn had seen her own car parked in her driveway that she had to laugh as she swept the key from his hand. Smiling, he opened the driver's door for her. She tossed her bag into the back and got in. By the time she had her seat pulled forward enough to reach the pedals, he'd come around and squeezed himself into the passenger seat.

"Good grief, who were you driving around before your engine conked?"

She chuckled as he let the seat back as far as it would go. "No one."

"No one must be short."

Grinning, she started the engine then paused to marvel at its silence. "It was never this quiet before."

"Well, it had problems."

She put the transmission in Reverse and backed it out of her drive. "The clutch is different."

"I adjusted it. The transmission should shift more smoothly now."

It took a few moments for her to acclimate herself to the new tension, but by second gear, she had it. "Very nice."

When the stop sign came within sight, she automatically shifted to a lower gear.

"Do you always downshift?"

Surprised by the question, she glanced at him. "Yes. The fellow who sold the car to me told me that I should."

"It's not bad advice," Jake said. "It's what I'd tell anyone driving a car with iffy brakes."

"You mean my brakes are bad?" she asked, dismayed at the possibility.

"Not anymore. As if I'd send you out in an unsafe vehicle."

She bit her lips but couldn't keep back a smile. "It wasn't part of our deal. The clutch, either."

"What's the difference? It needed to be done. I did it. Cost me nothing but time."

Maybe the added repairs had made no difference

in cost, but something had made a difference in him. She tried to keep her hope in check as she drove them through town, out onto the highway and to the ranch. No doubt his improved, more relaxed mood was the product of having finished, at long last, the repairs to her car. She didn't dare think that it could be anything else. She told herself to guard her heart, but a relaxed, congenial Jake was difficult to resist, and the longer he hung around, the more difficult—and alarming— it was.

She couldn't help wondering why, after avoiding her like the plague, he suddenly seemed to seek out her company. Monday, it was the car. On Tuesday, he told her that Frankie wanted her to watch him ride his pony again.

"We're headed to the barn. Won't you come out with us?"

Frankie jumped up and down in excitement. "Yeah, KKay, come out!"

Jake's mercurial moods were troublesome, but she couldn't say no, and the trip to the barn proved very enlightening. Jake introduced her to the other mounts in the stable before giving her a detailed tutorial on saddling a horse. Watching little Frankie fearlessly clean his pony's hooves was eye-opening. And terrifying. Kathryn managed to keep her mouth shut only because Frankie displayed an expertise and familiarity far beyond his years. The twinkle in Jake's eyes told her that he was well aware of her struggle, and that helped ease her fears, too.

"You know," Jake said, as he led the pony from the barn into the corral, "wouldn't hurt you to learn to ride."

Kathryn wasn't so sure about that. She glanced warily at the horses in the stalls behind her. They were enormous animals—beautiful but enormous. "Frankie," she asked, deadpan, "will you share your pony with me?"

Jake burst out laughing, though Frankie appeared to think it over before shaking his head. "You ride Mouse wif Daddy."

"Maybe Mouse is a better choice," she agreed, glancing at Jake, who had explained earlier that Mouse, a gelding, was named for the color of his coat, not his size. Mouse was huge, so riding lessons would have to wait until Kathryn gathered her courage. For riding and for trusting Jake again. Or maybe the issue was trusting herself. She didn't know anymore.

Frankie acquitted himself ably. He'd seemed well instructed before, but he was quite the little expert now. By the time they were all parched, Kathryn was suitably impressed. Jake sent her to the house to pour cold drinks for the three of them. After they'd cooled down, he kept her at the table for a good half hour, basically lecturing on horsemanship.

On Wednesday, as soon as Frankie went down for his nap, Jake asked Kathryn to take a look at his shop. He wanted advice on choosing paint colors and general organization, he said. Though afraid that her wariness concerning him was waning dangerously, she was too curious not to accompany him.

The shop walls were up, but the roof hadn't been put on yet, and windows and doors were missing. Jake pointed out the two pits where the lifts would go in the work bays and the four spaces in the blocks that represented doorways into the customer area, as well as the small restroom in the back far corner of the customer area and the storage space next to it.

"I thought the cash drawer and counter should go on this side next to the service bays, between the two doors. What do you think?" he asked.

"Hmm. Shouldn't the counter enclose that back door and access to the storage space? That way, you could come in directly from the service bay and everything could still be kept secure if you were here alone."

"Makes sense." He swept an arm to indicate another area. "What about the waiting area? What should I do there?"

She saw it all in her mind's eye. "Paint the floor black. Go army green about halfway up the wall, white over that with red and blue stars scattered everywhere. Paint your benches the same green as the wall."

Jake looked around as if picturing it all and broke out in a grin. "All right. What else?"

She paced off the length of the counter. "Put your coffee bar here and leave it open to both sides. That way, you can make fresh coffee from behind the enclosure." She pointed to the wall beside the restroom door. "Hang a TV right there."

He threw up his hands. "And *that's* why I brought you here. You have an uncanny ability to see how best to utilize spaces and put together colors. Have you ever thought of opening a decorating or consulting business?"

"Oh, no. I don't have the education."

"You can go to college online, you know."

"I can't afford that."

"But if there was a way, would you consider it?"

"I'd consider it," she said dismissively. But no way

existed, not until she could pay off her father. *If* she could pay off her father.

The rest of the week passed in similar fashion. Jake seemed to be around the house frequently. When he wasn't working on the shop, he was drinking glass after glass of iced tea at the kitchen table or helping Tyler and Frankie teach tricks to Tyler's dog, Tipper. Several times he sought out Kathryn to ask how her car was behaving or if she knew when to have the oil changed and how to check the tire pressure.

During his absences, Kathryn could easily remind herself that nothing had really changed. Jake might seem more relaxed and pleasant, even a little flirtatious at times, but neither of their situations had changed. He still had a business to establish and a late wife Kathryn knew she could never measure up to, and she had her father's claim hanging over her head. If she couldn't find a way to settle that, she'd be selling and moving because she certainly wasn't going to find anything to rent around here, or any other work that paid well enough to afford it.

By week's end, Kathryn very much feared she was well on her way to falling under Jake Smith's spell again, but she couldn't forget the pain of his indifference and the feeling of rejection. Could she bear that again? And again? Even if Jake decided that she would suffice as a girlfriend, who was to say that it wasn't a cycle she would have to endure from now on? She'd never survive a hot-and-cold Jake, content with her one minute, disappointed in her the next.

On Friday, she swallowed her building grief and applied for a position with every home care agency in the tri-county area. She'd take two jobs, if she could get them, and work day and night, seven days a week, until she had her father paid off. And Jake out of her heart.

Jake's heart sank when he saw Clark Goodell waiting in the church foyer that next Sunday. A quick glance around showed him that Kathryn had not yet arrived, but before he could get Frankie to the hallway that led to the children's wing, Goodell's face brightened. Jake could feel Kathryn's presence even before he turned to greet her, only to find her smiling at Goodell.

"I'm sorry I haven't called," Goodell said as soon as he reached her. "They've had me running all over the country."

"Oh, that's all right," she told him. "I understand. How was your trip?"

Frankie naturally headed in her direction. Jake caught him and tugged him down the hallway. "Hush now. We'll see Kathryn tonight. Remember? We're going over to the Pryors' for a cookout."

"S'let take KKay," Frankie said, staring wistfully behind him.

"That's exactly what we'll do," Jake answered.

Kathryn and Goodell were nowhere in sight when Jake returned to the foyer. Heavy of heart, he started down the aisle, spying them sitting side by side near the front and across the aisle from his family. He hadn't made arrangements with Kathryn to take her to the Pryors' tonight. He'd meant to do that this morning, to approach it as a given and simply ask her what time she wanted him to be there. Now he wished he'd done the thing properly and actually asked her to accompany him. Why was it, he wondered, that he could never seem to do the right thing with her?

He'd been a coward about her from the first. All along he'd told himself that he was just being prudent and fair. All the difficulties he'd used as excuses still applied, but he couldn't hide the truth from himself anymore. The way he felt about her scared him half to death. He'd already lost Jolene. The idea that he could go through that again…he couldn't think about it. Yet, he also couldn't let go of Kathryn.

Faith.

He had to trust that this was all happening for a reason. If only he didn't mess it up.

After the service, Jake hurried to the foyer, but instead of immediately going after Frankie, he hung around, chatting with one person or another, his hat in his hand, until Kathryn and Clark reached the already crowded space. Tina swung by on her way after Tyler and asked if Jake wanted her to pick up Frankie, too.

"That would be great. Thanks."

As soon as she disappeared down the hallway, he made his way over to Kathryn, who stood speaking to Clark and Wes Billings. Stepping up next to Kathryn, Jake took advantage of Billings's presence.

"Wes, you going to be joining us tonight?"

"You know it." Wes slid a glance at Clark, smiled and moved away, going to his wife, who stood laughing with some other women.

Fully aware that he'd rudely brought up a social engagement to which one of their party had not been invited, Jake felt a stab of guilt, but he wasn't backing down. He tried to think of the least objectionable way to accomplish his goal. It came in the form of his son, who suddenly appeared and threw himself at Kathryn.

"KKay! S'let go pardy now."

Jake chuckled. "That's not until tonight, son, and you've got to have a good, long nap first." He lifted a hand to the small of Kathryn's back, asking softly, "Can we pick you up about five-thirty?"

She glanced at Clark, color rising in her cheeks. "Oh, uh—"

"Earlier? Later?" Jake asked patiently.

Biting her lips, she glanced at Clark again then quickly, quietly said, "Five-thirty will be fine."

Smiling, Jake took Frankie by the hand, nodded at Clark and got out of there.

Would the day ever come, he wondered, when he could simply, formally ask the woman for a date? Maybe it was time to step up his game.

"Dese for you!" Frankie called, thrusting the bouquet of flowers at Kathryn with both hands.

As wide as he was, the colorful mixed blooms had been wrapped in the waxy, green paper that she recognized as coming from the local grocery. She'd never received flowers before, but then she'd never had so many invitations, either. First Jake, then Clark and two others, now Clark and Jake again. At least Clark had the good manners to make an actual request for her company. She just wished she could be as happy about that as she ought to be. Instead, it was Jake's high-handed assumption that she considered him her escort for the evening that both infuriated and thrilled her. The flowers just intensified the thrill.

Even if Frankie had delivered them, she had no doubt who had thought of and purchased them. He shouldn't have done it, not with the drain on his finances that the shop was making, but she couldn't be upset with him.

Her first date. Her first kiss. Her first flowers.

She didn't dare carry the thought further. She couldn't, wouldn't, let Jake Smith be her first love. If Jake was her first, she feared she would never know another. Taking the flowers in hand, she backed away from the door and smiled down at Frankie. She made a show of sniffing the blossoms.

"Mmm. Beautiful. Thank you so much."

Frankie swung his arms, obviously pleased with himself. "We gots 'em for Mizz Ann, too, an'…" He screwed up his face as if trying to remember. "Mizz Billie!"

"Donovan's great-grandmother," Jake informed Kathryn. "She lives with them."

"How very kind," Kathryn managed, busily tweaking one blossom after another. Finally, she looked at Jake.

He regarded her steadily, his hat in his hands, his folded sunshades poking up out of his shirt pocket. He'd shaved again since church, and her heart flip-flopped inside her chest. Flustered, she suddenly couldn't seem to breathe properly.

Oh, she was in trouble.

Big, big trouble.

Chapter Thirteen

Turning, Kathryn fled toward the kitchen, saying, "I'll put these in water and get the cake." Frankie ran for the sofa. Behind her, she heard Jake step into the house and close the door.

She was standing on a stool and pulling a vase down from an upper cabinet when Jake came into the kitchen. He tossed his hat onto the counter and reached around her, wrapping his long, strong fingers around the dusky green vase and taking it out of her hands. He stayed where he was as she backed down off the low stool. Slowly lowering the vase to the countertop, he momentarily surrounded her with his arms, his chest scant inches from her back. Kathryn closed her eyes, taking in the aroma and heat of him.

He smelled of shaving cream and mint, and though no part of him touched her, she felt warmed, embraced. After a moment, he backed away. Her heart hammering, she quickly turned to place the vase on the island beside the flowers and pulled open a drawer to find scissors.

"You could get the cake out of the fridge," she told

him, beginning to trim the flower stems. "I put it in there to set the icing."

Ann had tasked the Loco Man contingent with dessert for their cookout. Kathryn had proposed a strawberry cake. Tina had volunteered to provide homemade ice cream. Kathryn had placed the cake, on her mother's crystal cake plate, on the lowest shelf of the refrigerator. Bending, Jake carefully pulled it out.

"Wow. Chocolate-covered strawberries." He set the cake on the end of the island and licked a tiny blob of pink icing from his thumb. "Mmm, strawberry and cream cheese. Forget the steaks. This is my main course."

Dropping stems into the vase, Kathryn glanced at the cake, smiling. Chocolate-covered strawberries were her favorite indulgence. She'd covered the top of the cake with them. Jake apparently shared her affinity for the sweet, red fruit dipped in waxy chocolate.

"The cover is on the counter behind you."

He turned, spied the domed cake cover and picked it up by the glass knob on top. Carefully, he settled the glass dome over the cake. Folding his arms, he backed up to lean against the counter behind him and watched her arrange the flowers.

"That must be a new outfit you're wearing."

Keeping her head averted, she nodded and turned with the vase to carry it to the sink, where she began filling it with water. She'd told herself that her choice of deep, olive green had nothing to do with Jake's preference for army colors. Green, after all, was always her color of choice. She had passed over similar loose, comfortable capris and matching tops in two other shades of green, however.

"I like it," Jake said. "But then, you always look good, no matter what you wear."

Kathryn froze in the act of lifting the vase out of the sink, her pulse pounding. "Thank you." The words came out softer and more husky than she'd intended. Perhaps if she could breathe, she could speak normally.

Jake stepped up next to her and picked up the flowers. "Where would you like these?"

"I-island, for now." Later, she would move them to her bedroom, where she would see them the moment she awakened.

He carried the vase of flowers to the island and placed them in the center of the countertop before picking up his hat and fitting it to his head. "I'll get the cake."

Kathryn caught her breath and followed him into the living room. Frankie went nuts over the cake, hugging Kathryn and pretending to gobble the dessert with his hands.

"Um-um-um-um."

His antics eased Kathryn's hyperawareness of Jake. Laughing, they trooped out to the truck. Jake secured the cake in the back seat, and Frankie kept pretending to eat it as they drove to the Pryor farm. They were still getting out of the truck when Donovan Pryor and Tyler came running around the house. Donovan's red hair glowed like a flame against the sinking sun.

"We got ice cream!" Tyler called happily.

"An' cake!" Frankie shouted as Jake lifted him down to the ground. "Wif s'rawburries! Candy ones!"

"Strawberries," Donovan repeated, licking his lips. "Yum."

Jake handed Frankie the wrapped roses, and the boy ran toward the older ones, calling, "I gots flou-hers!"

Shaking his head, Jake instructed Frankie to deliver the roses. All three boys took off, yelling about strawberries, cake and flowers. Chuckling, Jake reached into the truck for the cake and carried it toward the house, Kathryn at his side.

"Looks like I'm going to have to fight off the hordes to keep my cake."

"*Your* cake?"

"My girl, my cake," he said silkily, dropping a warm, lazy look on her. Kathryn's heart stopped, her jaw dropping.

Before she could get her mouth closed, Dean Pryor, Ann's husband, came out onto the porch, calling to them. "Good to see y'all! Come on in." He reached for the cake as they climbed the steps, saying, "I'll take that."

"Oh, no, you won't," Jake said, twisting to keep the cake out of Dean's reach. "If you're real nice, I might let you have some, though."

Dean laughed. "It's like that, huh? I can see we're going to have to bribe you to share." Laughing, he pulled open the screen door for them.

"That might work," Jake conceded, winking at Kathryn. "Let's see what you've got to trade."

They walked through the old house, with its charmingly outdated furnishings and many family mementos, to the kitchen, where Ann and an older woman whom Dean quickly identified as his grandmother Billie were accepting Frankie's roses with smiles and exclamations of delight.

"KKay gots more," Frankie reported, holding his arms wide. "S'lot more. Huh, Daddy?"

"Lots more," Jake corrected, while Kathryn bit her lips to conceal a smile and tried to hide her blush.

"What's the occasion?" Ann asked.

Jake shrugged, grinning. "Steaks and strawberry cake. What else do you need?"

The two roses were deposited in matching vases and sent out the door with the boys and Dean.

Ann came and took the cake. "Thanks for the roses. That was so sweet. Oooh, the cake does look good. I'll put it over here next to the ice-cream freezer."

"I'm gaining weight just thinking about it," Tina drawled, entering the room from another part of the house.

"Me, too," Billie Pryor declared. "Let's get some exercise." She headed toward the door, waving for the others to follow. "I want to show y'all the garden before it gets dark, and I'll need some help gathering the corn."

Kathryn followed Billie and Tina out the back door, Jake on her heels. A couple of wood picnic tables, covered with checked plastic cloths, stood just beyond a large, shiny grill, where Ann's father, Wes Billings, tended a full grate of thick steaks while Dr. Alice arranged plates, napkins, flatware and plastic tumblers for iced tea and lemonade. A bud vase with a single long-stemmed rose rested in the center of each table.

A cooler of ice squatted between two folding lawn chairs occupied by Rex Billings and Wyatt. Several other chairs stood beneath the overarching limbs of an enormous hickory tree. Dean Pryor rose from feeding wood to a fire in a hole in the ground. A grate covered the fire pit, and a large, heavy pot of water sat atop the grate. He walked over to a lawn chair next to Ryder beneath the tree and dropped down into it before picking up a tall tumbler of iced tea from the ground. He gulped down a long drink, then waved at Jake.

"Grab a glass and a chair."

Tina set off up a small rise after Dean's grandmother, who now carried a pair of baskets. Jake leaned close to Kathryn and whispered, "I'll save you a seat."

Her heart in her throat, Kathryn merely nodded and went after Tina. Behind her, she heard Ryder teasing Jake.

"Can't the woman even walk up a hill without you ogling her?"

Despite the burn in her cheeks, Kathryn couldn't help looking back. Jake stood right where she'd left him, watching her. He slid a finger around the front curve of his hat brim in a kind of salute. Despite telling herself that it didn't mean anything, Kathryn felt as if she could float up that hill.

To her surprise, Kathryn found Billie Pryor's vegetable garden to be very interesting, especially the part planted in straw bales. While Billie gently lectured on growing vegetables, Tina and Kathryn followed her to the cornfield and helped her look for the remaining ears of corn and snap them off the stalks. When Billie decreed that they'd gathered enough corn, they carried the ears toward a water bib, where the boys washed and stripped them. Soon the ears went into the big pot heating over the fire pit.

Kathryn felt uncomfortably warm, despite the slowly sinking sun. Tina fanned herself with her hand

and started toward the lawn chairs, saying, "I hear a tall, cold glass of iced tea calling my name."

"Funny, I thought that was my name I heard."

"If you did," Tina teased, tossing a grin over her shoulder, "it was Jake calling."

Kathryn caught her breath, but then all she could see was Jake smiling at her. Somehow, she managed to make it down the hill without breaking anything. Jake waved her over to a chair at his side. Conversation had already turned to Tina's plan to put in a vegetable garden at Loco Man Ranch.

"Dean will till the ground for us," Tina explained, Dean nodding in agreement. "We just have to decide where to put our garden plot. It should be close to the house. I was thinking out past the storm cellar." She turned to Kathryn. "What do you think?"

"Unless you're planning to take down trees, that's not much space," Kathryn said, saddened to think that she wouldn't be there to see the garden take shape. She dared not linger at the ranch with Jake in this happy mood. It was bad enough when he was ignoring or snapping at her, but this attentive, flirtatious Jake was a great danger to her heart, and now that her car had been returned to her, she had no excuse for staying on at Loco Man.

"We'd have to push into the pasture to enlarge the area otherwise," Tina mused.

"We've got two thousand acres, sweetheart," Wyatt said. "We can give up a few yards of pasture for a garden."

"But you'd have to deal with the barbed wire and the cattle, then," Kathryn pointed out.

"Don't worry about that, honey," Jake said casually.

"I'll build you a fence to keep the cattle out, one with no barbed wire."

That word, *honey*, exploded like a grenade in Kathryn's mind. Apparently, it had quite an effect on everyone else listening, too. She saw knowing smiles and glances being exchanged everywhere she looked. Her face flamed red, and a lump formed in her throat. Why now, when it was too late? She couldn't trust him, dared not trust that he'd always be this Jake. The one she couldn't seem to help loving.

As night fell and the food disappeared, along with copious amounts of tea and lemonade, laughter rang out and conversation spun from one subject to another. Katherine sat next to Jake and mostly just listened, wondering what it would mean to truly be Jake's girl. Delight followed by heartache followed by delight followed by heartache? Or love and security without fail?

Rex and Callie Billings created considerable excitement by announcing that they were expecting a third child. Kathryn saw Tina and Wyatt exchange glances and smiles. Rex and his family left soon after, Callie saying she was exhausted all the time in the early weeks of her pregnancies. Rex, an attorney as well as a rancher, explained that he had paperwork to catch up on and needed to get an early start.

Perhaps half an hour later, Frankie crawled up in Kathryn's lap and went to sleep on her shoulder. He was a lead weight against her chest, a sweaty one, but she held him close, treasuring the feel of him in her arms, until Jake rose a few minutes later and gathered up the boy.

"We should be going, hon. Way past his bedtime."

Those endearments seemed to roll off his tongue with careless ease lately. If only she could trust in them.

The party began to break up in earnest, with Tyler whining that he didn't want to go and Tina herding the exhausted six-year-old toward the front yard while Wyatt fetched the ice-cream freezer. Wes had cleaned the grill as soon as the last steak had come off it, so he and Alice began helping Billie carry leftovers into the kitchen. Ann brought Kathryn her cake plate and dome, clean now. The cake had been a big hit.

"I hate to leave you with a mess," Kathryn said.

"No, no. Dad and Alice will help us finish up while Billie gets the kids down for the night. We'll be done before you get home." She hugged Kathryn around the covered cake plate clasped to her chest, adding, "It's so good to have you in our lives again."

Even as she murmured her agreement, Kathryn wondered if she would see any of these people anymore after she stopped working for the Smiths.

They arrived at her home fifteen or twenty minutes later. Sucking in a deep breath, Kathryn started to thank Jake for the flowers and the evening, but he lightly pressed a finger to her lips, whispering, "Don't want to wake Frankie."

Twisting to look into the back seat, where Frankie slept with his head lolling to one side, Kathryn nodded and reached for the door handle. She was going to miss that little boy fiercely. Jake got out on his side and started around to meet her. He'd turned off the overhead light in the cab, so Frankie slept on.

She still cradled the cake plate and its cover in her lap. Jake took them from her, and she slid out onto the gravel of her drive. Jake carried the empty cake plate and its cover with one arm and hit the lock with the other hand before gently closing the door. They walked in silence to her front steps and climbed them to the porch.

Kathryn took out her keys and unlocked the front door. To her surprise, Jake brushed past her and set the cake plate on the small table just inside the door. Kathryn reached for the trio of light switches on the wall above the table, but Jake's hand got there first. Instead of turning on the living room lights, however, he turned off the porch light. Then, there in the open doorway, he pulled her into his arms.

She shouldn't do it. She knew she shouldn't do it, but a growing sense of urgency filled her, an impatience which she recognized despite never having felt it before this moment. This was the end, her final chance to feel his arms around her. Turning up her face, she slid her arms around his neck and kissed him.

After the first time, she hadn't imagined that his kisses could improve, but she found herself moved in profound ways. This kiss shifted her reality.

She was lost now. She had no choice but to love him.

Sadly, it changed little. Just her.

Only his kiss could simultaneously ground her and fling her to the stars.

Only his kiss.

And this was the last one.

Jake woke early on Monday morning, as usual. He shaved, slipped downstairs and made coffee, but he didn't go to the shop. He wanted to see Kathryn as soon as she came in. After last night, she had to know how he felt about her. They had to talk things through and make a plan. He wanted a bit of privacy, not too much, just enough time to say the things he'd been contemplating. But not enough to allow temptation to get the better of him. The woman was a major temptation to him, though he hadn't wanted to admit it at first.

He'd realized, just before he'd drifted off to sleep, that he'd gotten so good at pushing away what seemed to weaken or threaten him that it had become second nature. With Jolene, he'd had to do it. No one could live in constant fear of losing someone they loved. Everyone had to find a way to cope with the threat of danger. His way was to deny his fears and refuse to think of them. He'd done the same thing with Kathryn. But it hadn't worked.

His feelings for her were stronger than his fear. No matter how hard he'd tried, he couldn't stay away from her. All he'd done was make himself miserable. Eventually, though, he'd seen her hidden strength and independence.

Despite her natural reticence and caution, she'd soldiered on in the face of tremendous difficulty. Her strength was born of love combined with generosity and personal sacrifice. She'd closed out a world that preached self-fulfillment, dependence and monetary success and done the right, best thing, even when all she'd had wasn't truly enough. In the process, she'd honed astounding talents, using them to create comfort, warmth and peace. The woman hadn't been inside a church for years, but she'd walked in and taken her place with the Smiths more of a Christian than anyone Jake knew, himself included. She humbled him. He could only pray that she'd forgive him.

A phone rang. Jake ignored it. A few minutes later,

Tina stumbled into the kitchen, Wyatt following in his bare feet, jeans and an undershirt. Jake didn't realize anything was wrong until she started sobbing. He jumped to his feet.

"What's happened?"

"She quit!" Tina exclaimed.

"What?"

"Kathryn quit. She said she's moving."

Astounded, he could think of only one question. "But why?"

Tina swiped tears from her face and folded her arms. "Think about it. I expect you'll figure it out."

"Me? Because of me?"

She threw up her hands. "What else?"

Jake didn't even try to answer that. Instead, he whirled and hit the door, leaving his hat behind. Maybe five minutes later, he whipped the truck into her drive, killed the engine and bailed out, the keys still in the ignition. Just as he raised his fist to knock on her door, he heard an unfamiliar voice, a masculine one, raised in what sounded like anger.

"Don't pretend I'm being unreasonable! You slaved for your mother but can't even share anything with me!"

"I offered you monthly payments," Kathryn said in a tired voice.

"I don't need monthly payments! I need a lump sum. Now!"

"I told you I'd sell the house," Kathryn said tremulously. "That's all I can do."

Sell her house? Jake opened the door without knocking and walked inside, confused and struggling not to rush to her aid without all the facts. One of the hallmarks of Kathryn's character was her calm, deliberate, careful manner. He would try to follow her lead in this, at least until he found out what was going on.

Her head turned at the sound of the door. Sadness mixed with resignation weighted her expression. She sat in the armchair, her entire body drawn into a tight, wary stillness, while a large, intimidating, middle-aged man with an unkempt mop of faded, thinning hair stood over her, bent forward slightly, his thick hands coiled into fists. One of those beefy fists clutched a sheaf of papers.

Jake's first instinct was to knock the bully over, but something, perhaps the dullness of Kathryn's eyes, told him that would be a mistake. She looked ready to shatter. He went to stand beside her chair.

"Honey, what's happening?"

"This isn't your business," the man growled. "Whoever you are, get out. This is between me and my daughter."

Daughter.

It was as he thought. Still, the word jolted Jake. He looked into the angry face of the long-absent Mitchel Stepp, seeing nothing of Kathryn in the bloated eyes, veined nose and heavy jowls.

Laying his hand on Kathryn's shoulder, Jake squeezed, letting her know that she wasn't alone.

If it were up to him, she would never be alone again.

But first things first. One problem at a time.

Faith.

They would work it out. God would help them work it out.

Chapter Fourteen

"Anything that concerns Kathryn concerns me," Jake said calmly. "And my family."

"I don't know you, and I don't care who your family is," Mitchel Stepp sneered.

"Jacoby Smith," Jake said, not bothering to offer his hand.

"Smith," the older man repeated in a considering tone. "There's that Smith on Loco Man Ranch. What's his name? Dodge?"

"Dodd. He was my uncle."

"Was." Suddenly, Mitchel Stepp's belligerence faded somewhat. "Old Dodd is gone, then, and you got the ranch."

"Me and my brothers," Jake clarified.

"He's not giving you money," Kathryn stated firmly.

Mitchel shook the papers at her. "Someone's giving me money! My lawyer says so! I can sell this house on my own, you know. My name's on the deed, not yours."

"Mother's will—" Kathryn began.

"Gives you half. That's all. Just half. And probating

that will to get your name on the deed will cost you a pretty penny. Save us both all the trouble."

Kathryn swallowed, her gaze dropping to the floor. "I said I'd sell the house."

"Oh, no, you won't," Jake declared, tightening his hand on her shoulder. "Not until we talk to our lawyer."

Kathryn tilted her head back, looking up at him. "*Our* lawyer?"

Jake dropped to his haunches, bringing his face close to hers. "Sweetheart, the ranch keeps Rex Billings on retainer. He's a fine lawyer and a good friend. I know he'll help us."

He leaned forward and kissed her forehead before pushing up to stand and again face Mitchel Stepp. "We'll talk to our lawyer and get back to you."

"Don't waste your money on lawyers. No lawyer's going to tell you anything I haven't already," Mitchel insisted. He smacked the papers in his hand with the other. "I got it all right here. Sell and be done!"

Biting her lips, Kathryn looked up at Jake. "I guess it can't hurt just to talk to Rex."

"That's my girl."

Tears filled her eyes. She looked tired enough to pass out where she sat.

"Time for you to go," Jake said to Mitchel Stepp. Leaving Kathryn's side, he pushed the older man toward the door.

"Get your hands off me!" Stepp blustered, smacking Jake with the papers in his fist.

Jake snatched the papers out of Mitchel's hand and stuffed them into the back pocket of his jeans. Mitchel tried to retrieve them.

"Give me those!"

"Not on your life. These are going to our lawyer," Jake decreed, hustling the man out the door. "I'm sure you've got copies."

Mitchel blustered and balked and glared, but he quickly stood on the porch looking in. Jake closed the door in Mitchel's face and threw the dead bolt. Then he simply turned to Kathryn, who surged to her feet. He opened his arms, and she flew to him. Folding her close, he tucked her head beneath his chin.

"It's okay, honey. It's all going to be okay."

"I don't know. I just don't know."

"We'll get through this together. All of us. You're not alone. Remember that."

She bowed her head. "Didn't Tina tell you?"

"That you quit? Yeah, she told me. But it isn't so. You know it isn't so. You just said that because you thought you were going to have to sell your house and move away."

"Jake," Kathryn whispered, "you should know—"

"If it's about the job, Kathryn, we'll discuss it later. Right now, we've got to figure out this mess with the house. Let me call Rex."

Disentangling himself, he took out his phone. Meanwhile, Kathryn went to the window and peeked through the sheers.

"Someone was waiting close by," she murmured. "They're picking him up now."

"Good riddance," Jake said just as Callie answered the call. After hearing why they wanted to consult Rex, she advised them to come over right away. "We'll be there in fifteen minutes or less," Jake replied before breaking the connection. "Can your father get into the house?" Jake asked Kathryn, looking for his hat.

"No. I had the locks changed about a month after he left. He'd been taking anything of value for years to buy his booze. One day after he disappeared, an oxygen tank went missing. I couldn't take the chance he'd help himself to anything else. He'd have sold Mom's wheelchair if he could've gotten his hands on it."

"Addiction is a horrible thing," Jake said, touching his head and remembering that he'd left his hat at home. He patted the front pocket of his jeans, then threw the dead bolt and opened the door. "You drive, hon. I want to call Wyatt. My truck's behind your car. The keys are, uh, in the ignition."

Kathryn lifted her eyebrows at that but said nothing as she snagged her bag from the closet and went out the door. As she drove them through War Bonnet, at a decidedly more sedate pace than he had on his way to Kathryn's, Jake gave Wyatt a blow-by-blow recitation of Mitchel Stepp's words and manner.

"Jake," she began again as soon as he ended the call, "you really should know…" Breaking off, she bit her lips.

He reached across the divide between their seats and smoothed his hand over the back of her neck beneath her thick, silky hair. "You should know some things, too, honey, but we'll talk later. I promise."

She nodded, looking troubled. Jake wouldn't let himself think about what she might have to tell him. Whatever it was, they'd work through it. He would not, could not, believe that it might be insurmountable. That wasn't in the plan.

Impossible was never part of God's plan.

They made good time, but Wyatt was closer and beat them to Straight Arrow Ranch. Kathryn parked behind

Wyatt's truck at the side of the road, and the three of them walked through the trees to the front porch of the ranch house. It was newer by a few decades than either the house at Loco Man or the Pryors' farmhouse, but it wasn't exactly a modern structure. Callie greeted them at the door, looking wan and hollow-eyed, then quickly excused herself.

Rex came out of a room on the right of the foyer, a worried expression on his face. He glanced down the hallway in the direction Callie had gone then smiled at Jake, Kathryn and Wyatt. "Hey. Callie told me y'all were coming."

"We don't want to intrude," Kathryn said, watching Callie disappear through a doorway, "or keep you from other business."

He shook his head. "Naw, not a bit. I'm sticking close to the house for a while because Callie's just so sick with this baby. Dad and Alice are watching the other kids for us so she can get on top of this."

"Tina's having her issues, too," Wyatt commented, "but it's more the afternoons for her. I thought it was supposed to be morning sickness."

Kathryn turned on him in shock.

"Is Tina pregnant?" Jake yelped, his eyes wide.

Wyatt grimaced. "I wasn't supposed to say anything for at least another month."

"Oh, my word!" Kathryn exclaimed. No wonder Tina wouldn't buy any clothes for herself! And all that talk about gaining weight.

Jake clapped his brother on both shoulders. "That's excellent news!"

"Not to mention fast work," Rex chortled.

Grinning, Wyatt said, "Tina's going to kill me, but

how are you supposed to keep something like that to yourself?"

"She won't stay mad too long," Rex teased. "No more than seven or eight months, anyway. A word of advice—learn to change diapers with your eyes closed. Comes in handy in the middle of the night."

"Thankfully, we've got Kathryn to help shoulder that burden," Wyatt said, but then he frowned and turned to her. "I thought we did, anyway."

"We'll talk about all that later," Jake interjected. "Right now, Kathryn's got a crisis of her own to deal with."

"Come on into the office," Rex said. "I want all the details."

Wyatt went across the room and leaned against the windowsill while Kathryn and Jake sank into a pair of wood-and-leather chairs in front of Rex's battered old desk. Jake handed over the papers he'd taken from Mitchel. Rex settled behind the desk and looked them over while Kathryn succinctly explained the situation.

He pulled a sheet of paper out of those on his desk and handed it to Kathryn. "Is this an accurate copy of your mother's will?"

Kathryn scanned the paper, frowning. "Yes. There were several copies, but the last time I looked, I only found one."

Rex passed over some papers. "How about this?"

She recognized the insurance policy. "Thank God! I thought I'd lost those." She shoved the papers at Jake. "My father must've taken these before I had the locks changed."

"But why?" Jake asked, scanning the papers. "He's

not the beneficiary of either the will or the insurance, so what good would this do him?"

Rex spread his hands. "Spouses have certain entitlements in Oklahoma that no will can circumvent. Insurance isn't one of them, but he might not have known that. He might even have shown these to a lawyer, hoping to find a legal way to subvert Mia's wishes. Or he might've just wanted to check out how much Kathryn would get so he could hit her up for part of it. Kathryn was young, after all, and no one knew how long Mia would live."

"Glad I got these away from him," Jake said, laying the papers on the desk.

Kathryn shook her head. "He must've been upset when he realized the amount of the policy had been reduced. We did that because we couldn't afford the premiums. Mom's old boss arranged it so the policy was fully paid with the premiums she'd already sent in, but he retired and the agency had no record of the amendment. I thought I'd misplaced our copy, and the insurance company said they couldn't verify the changes or process payment without solid proof."

Rex folded his arms against the edge of the desk. "Whatever Mitchel's reasons for taking these, the bottom line doesn't change. The proceeds of the life insurance are yours. Period. Other items mentioned in your mother's will are yours. Furniture, household goods, bank accounts…"

"There was just enough in the bank to bury her," Kathryn said.

Rex nodded. "The house, I'm afraid, is half his. Even if they divorced, unless there was a property settlement, he's entitled to half the value of your house."

Kathryn sighed. "They didn't divorce. At least I don't think they did. She never got anything saying he'd divorced her."

"He likely wouldn't have chanced it if he had any hopes of contesting her will," Rex said.

"So what do we do?" Jake asked, taking Kathryn's hand in his.

"I'm sure he has legal counsel. Just the fact that he waited six months after your mother's death to make his first demand tells me that. He doesn't want to look too predatory."

"He looked plenty predatory this morning," Jake put in.

"Sounds like his patience has worn thin, so we negotiate," Rex said. "We try for a buy-out price that you can live with. And we cash in the insurance policy. Maybe he'll take that. Maybe he won't. But we'll cut the best deal we can."

Jake squeezed Kathryn's hand. She gently removed it and smoothed the edge of Rex's desk with her fingertips, thinking through Rex's advice.

"The insurance won't be enough," she predicted. "He told us he has a lawyer, so he knows everything you just told me. I'll have to sell the house."

Jake slid an arm across her shoulder. "No, honey. Wait. We can come up with the cash. I know we can. I have several thousand at my disposal. That and the insurance money ought—"

She cut him off. "What are you saying? I can't take your money. That's for the shop."

"You're more important than the shop," Jake said softly. "Saving your home is what matters now."

"Loco Man looks after its own," Wyatt interjected. "We have funds. We can handle this together."

Confused, Kathryn shot to her feet, moving away from Jake, who also rose. She'd had this all settled in her mind even before her father had shown up that morning. Selling the house was the only real option. The insurance money just meant that she could easily start over again somewhere else. Away from everyone and everything she loved. But how could she stay and die a little every day, watching Jake pull away from her again? In time, he'd find someone else, someone like Jolene. What would she do then? How would she live with that?

"I'm not part of Loco Man," she gasped, barely holding it together.

"Of course you are," Jake insisted, coming toward her. "A huge part."

She shook her head, backing away. "No. Not anymore."

Jake looked at Wyatt, as if for help. Then he rubbed a hand over his face and turned back to Kathryn. "I'm part of Loco Man," he said. "And you're part of me."

Kathryn folded her arms across her middle, shaking her head. Nothing made sense anymore. It hadn't since the first time Jake had kissed her. He reached out, and she backed up a step.

"Please don't." She could barely think as it was. If he touched her now, she'd lose her mind.

"Just listen to me," he said. "I can put off opening the shop for a few months. Or...or sell it to someone who can see it through."

"No!"

"I'll borrow money, then, take out a loan. I'll make

it work. But I can't let you lose your home, not when I can see what it's doing to you."

"Stop trying to rescue me! Don't you understand? It's not about the house. I just can't…" *Be around you anymore.* Having friends was wonderful, but it just wasn't enough with Jake. She turned to Rex. "Do whatever you think is best, but I'm calling a Realtor today."

"Kathryn, please."

She ignored him and addressed Wyatt. "Will you take me ho—" She gulped down a fresh spate of tears. "Back to the house, please."

Wyatt sent Jake a loaded look and nodded grimly. Kathryn turned and walked out of the room. Tears were dripping off her chin before she reached Wyatt's truck. He arrived a few seconds later and let her in.

Kathryn stared blindly out the window, keeping her face averted and swiping impatiently at her tears. They drove quite a while in silence before Wyatt said, "He just wants…he *needs* to help you, Kathryn."

"Everyone's hero," she remarked bitterly. "What happens when I don't need to be rescued?"

"Could be he'll need you to rescue him."

"How could I possibly ever do that?"

"You'd be surprised."

Kathryn sighed and laid her head against the window. "I used to wish for a surprise every now and then, anything but the same old same old. Now I just want a quiet, steady, peaceful life."

"You think you'll find that by selling your house and moving away?" Wyatt asked.

"No," she admitted after a moment. "I don't think I'll ever find that. But maybe at least the pain will stop."

"You pulled away from everyone and everything once before, Kathryn. Did that make the pain stop?"

She closed her eyes, so tired. "No."

Tina pointed an accusing finger. "You'd better fix this, Jake Smith, and fix it fast! You brought her here, and now we can't manage without her."

"If I just knew what to do," Jake said miserably, his head in his hands, elbows braced against the tabletop.

"You can convince her that you love her," Wyatt said, coming through the door.

Jake dropped his hands. "Don't you think she knows that?"

"I do not think she knows that," Wyatt stated flatly.

Angry at the way this whole morning had turned out, Jake shot to his feet, his chair screeching against the floor. "I told her that I was willing to give up the shop and go into debt to help her! Does she think I'd do that just out of the generosity of my heart?"

"Yeah," Tina said, folding her arms. "She does. She thinks you're the kindest, most generous man in the world. Or she did before you started treating her like a leper."

Rocked, Jake felt the color drain out of his face.

"Think about it," Ryder said from his seat at the table. "You rescued her from the side of the road, got her a job here, fixed her car for free. And as soon as all her troubles were taken care of, you treated her like the biggest inconvenience on the face of the earth."

"No. That's not what—"

"And as soon as she's in trouble again, off you go," Tina interrupted, "riding to the rescue. What's she supposed to think? That she'll have to run from one calamity to another to hold your attention?"

"She said it herself just now," Wyatt told him. "Everyone's hero. That's what she called you."

Jake passed a hand over his eyes. "I only want to be her hero, but how am I supposed to convince her of that?"

Tina shook her head, looking at Wyatt. "I thought she was the innocent and he was the one with the experience."

"How did you convince Jolene that you loved her?" Ryder asked.

"I didn't," Jake said. "We just sort of fell into it." He tried to think what to say, how to make Kathryn hear him, but his brain didn't seem to be working. He wasn't sure it ever would again. "I don't know how to make Kathryn listen to me now. I'm not sure she'll even open the door for me."

"Well, you'd better think of something," Tina muttered.

He closed his eyes, silently talking to God. *Is this the end? You have Jolene with You, so I know she's all right. But Kathryn is alone, and if she leaves here, she'll always be alone. And I'll always be alone because I don't know how I'm supposed to live without her now.*

Frankie came stumbling into the room just then, yawning and rubbing his eyes. "Where Ty'er?"

"The school bus picked him up, sweetie," Tina said. "Let me make you some breakfast."

Suddenly, Jake knew what to do. "We don't have time for that," he said, taking Frankie by the arm. "Go to the bathroom. I'll bring down your clothes."

"I'll get them," Tina said, her face brightening as Frankie shuffled off.

"I have something that might help," Wyatt told him. "Let me get it."

Jake nodded, not sure what Wyatt had in mind and not caring. "Ryder, can you find an apple or a cheese stick, something for Frankie to eat on the way?"

They all went in different directions. Tina returned with the clothes, and Jake quickly dressed Frankie.

"We goin', Daddy?"

"Yes, son. We're going after Kathryn."

Frankie smiled and let Jake lead him back to the kitchen, where Ryder waited with a cheese stick and slices of apple in a small plastic dish.

"Here you go, pard. Eat it slow."

"And this is for you," Wyatt said, handing Jake a small box.

"What's this?"

"Mom's engagement ring. It's too small for Tina's hand, and I hated to alter it, but I'm guessing it'll fit Kathryn."

Gulping, Jake opened the box. The diamond was middling, maybe just over half a carat, but the setting was elegant and the slender band platinum.

"You and Jolene bought a ring before we could offer it to you. Dad said God must have other plans for it."

"I hope so," Jake said in a thick voice, hugging his brother. He swept Frankie toward the door, but at the last second he paused and looked back. "Well, start praying. I need all the help I can get."

Chapter Fifteen

Boom. Boom. Boom.

Kathryn jerked at the sound of a fist applied to her door. She'd finally stopped crying long enough to look for the local real estate agent's number, and now this. If it was another man asking her out, she was going to bodily remove him from her porch; she didn't care if he wanted to take her to Buckingham Palace.

Boom. Boom. Boom. The sound came accompanied this time by lighter sounds that peppered the bottom of the door. What on earth? She finally got up and went to see.

"KKay!"

When she opened the door Frankie threw both arms around her, as usual, knocking her back a step. She glared at Jake. Oh, this was low, unforgiveable. To use his own child against her. What kind of complex drove a man to such extremes?

"I've made up my mind," she told him firmly. "I'm selling the house and leaving here."

"Okay," he said, crowding inside and forcing her back another step. He got her in far enough to reach behind him and close the door. "If that's what you want to do, we'll go with you."

"What?"

He rested his hands on Frankie's shoulders. "We'll go with you. Anywhere you want to go."

She stepped back out of Frankie's embrace. "I can manage by myself."

"I know. You always have. But I can't let you do it this time. I love you, Kathryn. And Frankie loves you, too. It'll kill me and break his heart if you leave here without us. Or if you stay without us."

He loved her? She was too stunned for a moment to do anything but stare. How could that be?

"What? Why? Why hold yourself back? Why make me think—"

"Fear," he admitted. "Sheer terror. I love you more than I've ever loved anyone, Kathryn, but I've been down this road before, and the thought of losing someone else I love…" He shook his head. "I was so afraid that I tried to keep my distance. I made up every excuse for it I could think of, but the truth is I knew… from the beginning, some part of me has known that if I loved you and lost you…" He spread his hands. "I don't know how to survive that. God forgive me, I don't know how I would survive that. My faith just isn't that strong. What I had to figure out is that losing you is losing you, no matter how it happens. But I'm not going to lose you because I was too stupid to tell you how much I love you."

She stared at him, hardly able to believe what she was hearing. Then the tears came again. She couldn't stop them. And with them came all the hope and trust she'd tried so hard to put away.

"Oh, Jake. I've loved you from the very start, and I hoped you might feel the same, but I didn't dare believe it."

He heaved a huge sigh and stepped to the side, reaching for her. "Thank God. Thank you, God." He pulled her against him.

"It hurt so much when you stopped being nice to me," she said into the hollow of his shoulder. "The silence and the distance. It was unbearable."

"Honey, I'm sorry. You don't know how sorry. If it's any consolation, I was utterly miserable the whole time. And I hated—hated—seeing you with those other men."

She bit her lips, and then she giggled, elation rising up within her at last. "That part was kind of fun," she admitted. Pulling back a few inches, she looked him in the eye, adding, "But none of them could measure up to you."

Smiling broadly, he cupped her face in his hands and kissed her. Suddenly so happy she couldn't contain herself, she started to laugh.

"Hey," Frankie said, elbowing his way between them. "S'that my KKay."

Grinning, Jake put a hand on his head. "Back out, buckaroo. I can handle it from here. And you have to learn to share."

Frankie stepped aside, but he folded his arms and frowned up at his father. Jake ignored him, reaching into his pocket. He pulled out a small box. Kathryn gasped.

"Hold on," he said, taking her hand and going down on one knee. "I've got to do at least one thing right in this cockeyed courtship."

"Jake!" She clapped her free hand over her mouth.

"Kathryn Kay Stepp," he said, smiling up at her, "will you marry me? Please?"

"Yes! Oh, yes!"

Rising, he grinned ear to ear and pulled the top off the little box. "It was my mother's. The diamond's not all that big, but—"

"It's beautiful."

"Let's hope it fits," he said, taking the ring from its bed of cotton. It slid onto her finger as smoothly as silk.

"Later, if you want to," he said, holding her hands and rubbing his thumbs over her knuckles, "we can get a bigger diamond."

She yanked her hand away. "No! It's perfect. Why would you alter something this precious? I won't let you ruin it."

Jake chuckled and wrapped his arms around her. "Kathryn, I love you more than life. Promise me you'll never change."

"You're going to make me cry again," she grumbled. "And of course I'll change. So will you. We'll change together. Until we morph into an old married couple who finish each other's sentences and…" She dissolved into tears again. "Oh, Jake, I'm so happy!"

How could she not be? A man who loved her. A man she loved. Family. Friends. Even a son.

As Jake kissed the tears away, grinning all the while, Frankie shoved in between them again.

"My KKay!"

Laughing, she wiped her face with both hands. "Yes. I'm your KKay." She put her hands on her knees, stooping enough to bring her face level with his. "But now I'm going to be your mommy, too. Is that all right?"

He looked at Jake as if to say, *Well, duh. Like I haven't known that all along.* Then he wrapped his little arms around her again, tilted his head back as far as it would go and very clearly said, "Mama, I'm hungry."

Kathryn and Jake both laughed. Reaching down, he caught Frankie beneath the arms and swung him up onto his hip.

"Neither of us have had breakfast."

She smiled. "I guess I'd better cook then."

As she turned toward the kitchen, Jake slung an arm around her neck, pulling her sideways so he could kiss her temple.

"Let's eat," he said. "Then let's figure out how to save our home."

She nodded, a lump forming in her throat. Suddenly, nothing seemed impossible. They'd figure this out. Together.

"What a ride," Wyatt said the next afternoon, looking at the ring on Kathryn's finger again.

Jake nodded. Yeah, it had been some roller coaster, but he couldn't be happier. Whatever happened, he and Kathryn would face it together. They'd shared their news with the rest of the family yesterday, then talked long into the night about what they hoped for and how many options they might have. He'd slept like a baby afterward, and Kathryn had said much the same thing when she'd come in this morning.

"I still haven't fully recovered from the heart attack you gave me when you called yesterday," Tina said to Kathryn. She pointed a finger at Jake. "If you hadn't fixed this, Jake Smith, you'd be living in the bunkhouse with him." She jerked her head at Ryder.

Jake looked at Kathryn, sure she was thinking the same thing he was. They might both wind up living in the bunkhouse. He hoped not, but he couldn't worry about it anymore. Kathryn was going to be his wife, and whatever happened, he would live in that joy. Besides, if God could arrange that, He could work out the rest of it. Jake just didn't want her to be unhappy if they had to sell the house, after all. As long as they were together, though, they'd be fine.

Kathryn got up from the table to start dinner, but a tap on the door turned her attention in that direction.

"That'll be Rex," Wyatt said, and it was.

Rex came in and hung his hat on a peg. Jake saw the way Kathryn stiffened, as if preparing herself for bad news. He got up and went to wrap his arms around her.

"You saw my father."

"Spoke with his attorney," Rex corrected. "After I did a little research."

"Oh?"

"Can I get you some tea, Rex?" Tina asked.

He shook his head. "Naw. This won't take long."

"Spit it out," Jake said. "We can take whatever you've got to say."

"Twenty-five thousand. He'll settle for twenty-five thousand."

Kathryn turned in the circle of Jake's arms and laid her head on his shoulder. It was less than they'd feared, but still more than they could pull together.

"That's all?" Jake asked, suspicious of the amount. "He'll sign over the deed for a buyout of twenty-five thousand dollars?"

"It doesn't make sense," Kathryn said. "He was so

adamant that I sell the house and split the proceeds with him."

"He has no choice," Rex divulged. "It's that or go to jail."

She whirled around. "Jail!"

"He's willing to take that now rather than wait for the house to sell," Rex explained, "because he has a judgment against him in Tahlequah. A restitution judgment. Seems he got drunk one night and entered the wrong house."

"He did that to our next-door neighbor!" Kathryn exclaimed. "Nearly scared her to death. She still hasn't forgiven him."

"Well, this time the homeowner pressed charges. Apparently, there was considerable damage—broken door and windows, some lamps and furniture. And he owes attorney fees. If he doesn't pay up, he goes back to jail, and I'm sure he's running out of time."

"That explains a lot," Jake said. It did, indeed, not that it mattered. It was what it was, and they would deal with it. "The bank should be able to loan us that much, especially if we put down the insurance money."

"Without a steady income?" Kathryn asked softly.

"That's not a problem," Wyatt said.

"We've got income," Jake pointed out, focused on Kathryn. "The ranch makes money, and if the shop turns a profit, we'll have no worries."

"I'll get a job," she said.

"You've already got a job," Tina told her, but Kathryn had told Jake that she couldn't accept money from family for just helping out around the place.

"I've already applied at all the home care agencies," Kathryn went on. "One of them will call."

"Will you two shut up for a minute and let somebody else get a word in edgewise?" Tina demanded.

They pulled apart, staring at her in surprise. She walked over to Wyatt and linked her arm with his. "Jake," she said rather primly, "Wyatt and I have discussed this thoroughly, and we've agreed. You and Ryder have done a lot of work on *my* house. I owe you both."

"Don't be silly. I live here, and we agreed at the beginning that Ryder and I would work on the house in exchange for room and board."

"That was before I married your brother," Tina insisted.

"And truth be told," Wyatt put in, "the division of income we agreed to at that time is unfair, and we knew it even then. Tina and I shouldn't get half while you and Ryder each get a fourth."

"But there are four of us in this," Jake argued.

"And soon there will be five," Wyatt countered, pointing at Kathryn. "And one day there will be six. No, the only way to do this fairly is a one-third split for each of us brothers."

"And the wives share in the husbands' split," Tina said. "Simple."

"That being the case," Wyatt pronounced authoritatively, every inch the big brother now, "we've put cash aside for you and Ryder. You don't have to dip into your savings, and Kathryn doesn't have to give up her insurance money. It's covered, the full amount."

Stunned, Jake walked slowly across the floor and brought his hands up to rest on his brother's broad shoulders. "Wyatt, I love you and Tina for this, but I can't take your money."

"It's *your* money!" Tina exclaimed. "We were going to surprise you with it when you opened the shop. As for Ryder, we kind of figured he might want to buy his own vehicle. We just didn't want to ruin the surprise by giving him his cash before you got the shop open."

"By the way," Wyatt said, "we've got another sod harvest coming up, and that's another infusion of income that will more than see us all through the winter. Not that we were worried about it at all."

Jake looked at Kathryn. He ran his hand through his hair.

"I don't know what to say."

"I do," Kathryn spoke up. "Thank you. And thank God!" She burst into noisy sobs then.

Jake hurried to gather her against him, chuckling softly. "Oh, honey, don't cry now that everything's fine."

"I've cried more since I got happy than I ever did before," she wailed. "I just can't help it." Sniffing, she looked up at him then. "Thank God you stopped that day. Thank God I found enough courage to go with you." She looked around the room, as if memorizing the moment and every face.

Jake heard Frankie and Tyler laughing upstairs. He tried to see it and hear it as she did. Frankie, who had loved and wanted her from the beginning. And Wyatt, who was the best big brother in the world. And Tina, the sister Kathryn had never had. Ryder, the big old teddy bear. He was right. Their mom would approve. Jake silently vowed to spend the rest of his life making Kathryn so happy they'd have to buy tissues by the truckload.

"I have a family," Kathryn said softly, looking over his shoulder. "And I love you all so much."

Tina rushed them, hugging both Kathryn and Jake, while Wyatt looked on, grinning. Rex crossed the room and reached for his hat.

"Time to go check on my wife."

He turned a bright smile on them and went out the door while they were still thanking him.

Kathryn laid her head on Jake's shoulder. "Thank You," she whispered. "Thank You. Thank You. Thank You."

Jake knew she wasn't thanking him, and that was just as it should be.

"Amen," he whispered.

Jake waited in front of the altar in a brand-new suit. His boots gleamed, and the green tie Kathryn had picked out for him perfectly matched the dresses that Tina, Ann and Meredith wore. Jake had tapped Ryder as his best man because Wyatt had landed the privilege of escorting Kathryn down the aisle.

Despite his misgivings, they'd decided to invite Mitchel to the wedding, but he hadn't bothered even to respond to the invitation. Jake was relieved, and if Kathryn was not, at least she wasn't upset. Her father hadn't been part of her life in a long while, after all.

Rex Billings and Dean Pryor made up the rest of the wedding party, along with Frankie as ring bearer, Tyler as candle lighter and three little flower girls in identical flowered dresses. Dr. Alice herded her granddaughters toward the front of the church. Halfway down, the littlest one turned and demanded to be held. Muted laughter circled the room. Alice picked up the child and carried her to Wes, while the eldest, Callie's daughter, calmly urged her remaining cousin down the aisle, scattering petals as they went.

Jake couldn't smile any wider. October was a good month to get married. The weather had cooled and the leaves had begun to turn. They'd had time to decorate Frankie's room at the house in town, stenciling puppies on the walls.

Stark had finally pronounced Frankie's pup old enough to leave his mom. Tufts, so named for the tufts of hair on the top of his head and end of his tail, had developed a particular fondness for Kathryn. Who didn't? She'd turned out to be a very able trainer.

Jake wasn't surprised. He firmly believed she could do anything she put her mind to, including make her own wedding dress. She'd insisted, claiming that she couldn't find what she wanted in the stores. He thought she just hadn't wanted to spend the cash. She hadn't learned how to have money yet, or so she said.

She proved once again just how talented she was as soon as the doors opened at the back of the sanctuary. A strapless sheath of white satin overlaid with long sleeves, an off-the-shoulder neckline and a modest train in pure white lace, the dress could not have been more perfect. Her hair was long enough now to be twisted up in a sophisticated French roll, showing off her beautiful neck and collarbone. Wyatt had once deemed her plain, but she looked like a model today, with a bouquet of bright orange roses, the finest of veils flowing down her back and her lovely face smiling at him.

It was all Jake could do to wait for her to reach him. He was ready to start this life as husband and wife. More than ready. But they had the ceremony to get through first and a reception at Loco Man, with a huge cake baked by Callie Billings and decorated with strawberries dipped in white chocolate. He was delaying the opening of the shop for another week so they could take a honeymoon. His worries on that end had dissipated like so much smoke. He already had more work lined up than he could handle and was looking for a mechanic to hire.

They were headed to Galveston on their honeymoon. Thankfully, Frankie was not a fan of the beach. He'd had enough of it while they were in Houston, apparently. He was content to stay at the ranch for a few days with Tyler and his pup and his pony. Jake would show Kathryn his old stomping grounds and they'd have time alone together, just the two of them.

Perfect. It was all so perfect. She was perfect, or as close as a human being could get.

"Wow," he said, as soon as she reached him.

Their guests laughed, and she blushed, but then her hand was in his, and they were standing in front of the minister. Tina held the bouquet along with her own at exactly the right angle to disguise her baby bump. Ryder helped Frankie deliver the rings, and the next thing Jake knew, he was married. He thought of Jolene and how happy she had made him. He couldn't have been more grateful, but he knew that had just been the prologue for now.

He held Kathryn in his arms, looked down into her beautiful, serene face—this wife of his, the mother his son had chosen, the mother of his future children, the constant source of his delight—and softly said, "I love you."

"I love you, too," she said, loud enough for everyone in the building to hear, and then she kissed him.

His shy, proud, stubborn, talented, beautiful wife kissed him. Until his precocious, self-assured, somewhat territorial son yelled, "Hey! S'that my KKay!"

Laughter, it turned out, was the perfect recessional for a completely joyous occasion.

* * * * *

If you loved this story,
check out the first book from
Arlene James's miniseries
Three Brothers Ranch

The Rancher's Answered Prayer

Or pick up these other stories of ranch life
from the author's previous miniseries
The Prodigal Ranch

The Rancher's Homecoming
Her Single Dad Hero
Her Cowboy Boss

Available now from Love Inspired!

Find more great reads at www.LoveInspired.com

Dear Reader,

How difficult it is to remain obedient in the face of apparent calamity! Yet, obedience is exactly how we should respond when things look most dire. Sometimes the only way to remain obedient seems to be to withdraw from the world around us. That was Kathryn's reaction when an accident made an invalid of her mother.

Perhaps it doesn't occur to us—perhaps it shouldn't—that God will use our obedience to bring many blessings into even the most hopeless situation, but that's exactly what He does. Likewise, He uses difficulty to build strength in us, strength of character, strength of faith. When Jake understands that more than one kind of strength exists, he finds the courage to love again.

Fortunately, we don't have to find obedience or strength within ourselves. God is always there, always working on our behalf. May you always hold to Him, our shield and salvation.

God bless,
Arlene James

COMING NEXT MONTH FROM
Love Inspired®

Available March 19, 2019

THE AMISH SPINSTER'S COURTSHIP
by Emma Miller
When Marshall Byler meets Lovey Stutzman—a newcomer to his Amish community—it's love at first sight. Except Lovey doesn't believe the handsome bachelor is serious about pursuing her. And with his grandmother trying to prevent the match, will they ever find their way to each other?

THEIR CONVENIENT AMISH MARRIAGE
Pinecraft Homecomings • by Cheryl Williford
The last thing widowed single mother Verity Schrock expects is to find her former sweetheart back in town—with a baby. Now the bishop and Leviticus Hilty's father are insisting they marry for their children's sake. Can a marriage of convenience cause love to bloom between the pair again?

THE RANCHER'S LEGACY
Red Dog Ranch • by Jessica Keller
Returning home isn't part of Rhett Jarrett's plan—until he inherits the family ranch from his father. Running it won't be easy with his ranch assistant, Macy Howell, challenging all his decisions. But when he discovers the truth about his past, will he begin to see things her way?

ROCKY MOUNTAIN DADDY
Rocky Mountain Haven • by Lois Richer
In charge of a program for foster youths, ranch foreman Gabe Webber is used to children...but fatherhood is completely different. Especially since he just found out he has a six-year-old son. Now, with help from Olivia DeWitt, who's temporarily working at the foster kids' retreat, Gabe must learn how to be a dad.

HER COLORADO COWBOY
Rocky Mountain Heroes • by Mindy Obenhaus
Socialite Lily Davis agrees to take her children riding...despite her fear of horses. Working with widowed cowboy Noah Stephens to launch his new rodeo school is a step further than she planned to go. But they might just discover a love that conquers both their fears.

INSTANT FATHER
by Donna Gartshore
When his orphaned nephew has trouble at school, Paul Belvedere must turn to the boy's teacher, Charlotte Connelly, for assistance. But as the little boy draws them together, can Paul trust Charlotte with his secret...and his heart?

LOOK FOR THESE AND OTHER LOVE INSPIRED BOOKS WHEREVER BOOKS ARE SOLD, INCLUDING MOST BOOKSTORES, SUPERMARKETS, DISCOUNT STORES AND DRUGSTORES.

LICNM0319

Get 4 FREE REWARDS!

We'll send you 2 FREE Books plus 2 FREE Mystery Gifts.

Love Inspired® books feature contemporary inspirational romances with Christian characters facing the challenges of life and love.

Their Family Legacy
Lorraine Beatty

The Rancher's Answered Prayer
Arlene James

FREE
Value Over **$20**

They'd both just turned back to their work when a familiar loud, croaking sound cut the silence.

The twins shrieked and ran from where they'd been playing into the little cabin's yard and slammed into Anna, their faces frightened.

"What was that?" Anna sounded alarmed, too, kneeling to hold and comfort both girls.

"Nothing to be afraid of," Sean said, trying to hold back laughter. "It's just egrets. Type of water bird." He located the source of the sound, then went over to the trio, knelt beside them, and pointed through the trees and growth.

When the girls saw the stately white birds, they gasped

"They're so pretty!" Anna said.

"Pretty?" Sean chuckled. "Nobody from around here would get excited about an egret, nor think it's especially pretty." But as he watched another one land beside the first, white wings spread wide as it skidded into the shallow water, he realized that there was beauty there. He just hadn't noticed it before.

That was what kids did for you: made you see the world through their fresh, innocent eyes. A fist of longing clutched inside his chest.

The twins were tugging at Anna's shirt now, trying to get her to take them over toward the birds. "You may go look as long as you can see me," she said, "but take careful steps by the water." She took the bolder twin's face in her hands. "The water's not deep, but I still don't want you to wade in. Do you understand?"

Both little girls nodded vigorously.

They ran off and she watched for a few seconds, then turned back to her work with a barely audible sigh.

"Go take a look with them," he urged her. "It's not every day kids see an egret for the first time."

"You're sure?"

"Go on." He watched her run like a kid over to her girls. And then he couldn't resist walking a few steps closer and watching them, shielded by the trees and brush.

The twins were so excited that they weren't remembering to be quiet. "It caught a *fish*!" the one was crowing, pointing at the bird, which, indeed, held a squirming fish in its mouth.

"That one's neck is like an S!" The quieter twin squatted down, rapt.

Anna eased down onto the sandy beach, obviously unworried about her or the girls getting wet or dirty, laughing and talking to them and sharing their excitement.

The sight of it gave him a melancholy twinge. His own mom had been a nature lover. She'd taken him and his brothers fishing, visited a nature reserve a few times, back in Alabama where they'd lived before coming here.

Oh, if things were different, he'd run with this, see where it led…

Don't miss
Lee Tobin McClain's Low Country Hero,
available March 2019 from HQN Books!

www.Harlequin.com

PHLTMEXP0319

Looking for inspiration in tales
of hope, faith and heartfelt romance?

Check out **Love Inspired**® and
Love Inspired® **Suspense** books!

New books available every month!

CONNECT WITH US AT:

Facebook.com/groups/HarlequinConnection

 Facebook.com/HarlequinBooks

Twitter.com/HarlequinBooks

 Instagram.com/HarlequinBooks

 Pinterest.com/HarlequinBooks

ReaderService.com

Love Inspired.

LIGENRE2018R2

SPECIAL EXCERPT FROM

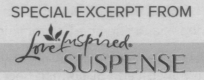

When K-9 administrative assistant Sophie Jordan sees
someone tampering with her boss's notes, she finds
herself in a killer's crosshairs. Can NYPD K-9 cop
Luke Hathaway and his partner keep her safe?

Read on for a sneak preview of
Justice Mission by Lynette Eason,
the thrilling start to the True Blue K-9 Unit series,
available in April 2019 from Love Inspired Suspense!

Get away from him.

Goose bumps pebbled Sophie Jordan's arms, and she
turned to run. The intruder's left hand shot out and closed
around her right biceps as his right hand came up, fingers
wrapped around the grip of a gun. Sophie screamed when
he placed the barrel of the weapon against her head. "Shut
up," he hissed. "Cooperate, and I might let you live."

A gun. He had a gun pointed at her temple.

His grip tightened. "Go."

Go? "Where?"

"Out the side door and to the parking lot. Now."

"Why don't you go, and I'll forget this ever happened?"

"Too late for that. You're coming with me. Now move!"

"You're *kidnapping* me?" She squeezed the words out,
trying to breathe through her terror.

Still keeping his fingers tight around her upper arm, he gave her a hard shove and Sophie stumbled, his grip the only thing that kept her from landing on her face.

Her captor aimed her toward the door, and she had no choice but to go. Heart thundering in her chest, her gaze jerked around the empty room. No help there. Maybe someone would be in the parking lot?

Normally, her penchant for being early averted a lot of things that could go wrong and usurp her daily schedule. Today, it had placed her in the hands of a dangerous man—and an empty parking lot in Jackson Heights. Where was everyone?

Think, Sophie, think!

A K-9 SUV turned in and she caught a glimpse of the driver. Officer Luke Hathaway sat behind the wheel of the SUV. "Luke!"

With a burst of strength, she jabbed back with her left elbow. A yell burst from her captor along with a string of curses. She slipped from his grip for a brief second until he slammed his weapon against the side of her head.

Don't miss
Justice Mission *by Lynette Eason,*
available April 2019 wherever
Love Inspired® Suspense books and ebooks are sold.

www.LoveInspired.com

Love Inspired®

**Inspirational Romance to
Warm Your Heart and Soul**

Join our social communities to connect
with other readers who share your love!

Sign up for the Love Inspired newsletter
at **www.LoveInspired.com** to be the
first to find out about upcoming titles,
special promotions and exclusive content.

CONNECT WITH US AT:

Facebook.com/groups/HarlequinConnection

 Facebook.com/LoveInspiredBooks

 Twitter.com/LoveInspiredBks